The Mythopoeic Society
1967 · Fiftieth Anniversary · 2017
50

The Mythic Circle

#42: 2020

Victoria Gaydosik
Manager and Fiction Editor

Nolan Meditz
Poetry Editor

Gwenyth Hood
Editor Emerita

Phillip Fitzsimmons
Archivist

Table of Contents

Access the audio files mentioned above for free at the Digital Archives of The Mythic Circle *after August 1, 2021, at* https://dc.swosu.edu/mcircle/ *or purchase a copy at* http://www.mythsoc.org/mythic-circle.htm.

The Mythic Circle

#42: 2020

Information for Aspiring Contributors

The Mythic Circle solicits original fantasy-inspired stories and poems from the membership of the Mythopoeic Society and from the larger world—anyone may contribute, but we give first consideration to our membership. We are also looking for original visual art contributions in the form of jpeg or other suitable file formats.

A small literary magazine, *The Mythic Circle* is published electronically and for print-on-demand by the **Mythopoeic Society**, an organization which celebrates the work of J. R. R. Tolkien, C. S. Lewis, and Charles Williams. These innovative writers drew upon the rich tradition of imaginative speculative narratives and returned fantasy to a respectable place in serious literature, and we carry on in their tradition. An affordable annual membership in the Society is available at http://www.mythsoc.org/join.htm.

The editors look mostly for original work by authors following the mythic tradition; this *can* include a certain amount of commentary and allusion to the works of other mythic authors (though such allusions and commentary are not necessary). However, the editors do not wish to see "fan fiction" such as stories that make use of characters, settings, or images from works by living or recent authors or artists or any works still under copyright.

Submissions and letters of comment should be e-mailed to mythiccircle@mythsoc.org. Contributors may also join the SWOSU Digital Commons, the archival repository of the Mythopoeic Society, and use the submission portal there, located at the following URL: https://dc.swosu.edu/cgi/submit.cgi?context=mcircle. Joining the Digital Commons will also provide extensive statistical feedback to contributors about worldwide downloads.

Editors' Introductions

The Mythic Circle is a creative writing journal devoted to fantasy-inspired creative works; it has been published by the Mythopoeic Society since 1987, and earlier versions of the Society's creative writing efforts extend to *Mythril* (1971 to 1980) and *Mythellany* (1981 to 1987). These journals have now been archived in their entirety at https://dc.swosu.edu/mythsoc/ through the efforts of the Society's archivist, Phillip Fitzsimmons, and digital assistant Benjamin Dressler. All but the current issue may be downloaded for free, and the current issue may be purchased as a digital download or ordered as a print-on-demand title from Amazon.

In its thirty-three year existence, *The Mythic Circle* has benefitted from the creative efforts of a wide variety of authors and artists, and some have been repeat contributors, including some who have written for this issue: Joe R. Christopher, author of the Arthurian dialog "Six Years After the Wedding," contributed to the very first issue of *The Mythic Circle*; S. Dorman, author of "Working Title," imagining a conversation between C. S. Lewis and Mark Twain, contributed two stories to the second issue; David Sparenberg, author of the poem "Ritual," became a contributor with several poems in Issue #11; Lee Clark Zumpe, author of the dragon tale "The Dreaded Tome of Urawn," first appeared in Issue #15; Kevan Bowkett, author of "Troll," first contributed a poem to Issue #37; Holly Day's first poems for us appeared in Issue #40, Lawrence Buentello and Meg Moseman joined us just last year, and all of these authors have made subsequent contributions after their first. We have deep connections like these with many additional authors.

But we also welcome new voices, such as Mary Alice Dixon, author of the folktale "The Tree That Stood Forever," Ella Wallsworth-Bell, author of the fantasy romance "Falling for a Cornish Maid," Ama Kirchner, author of "What Iphigenia Knows," drawn from Greek mythic roots, and DC Mallery, author of "Equuleus of Troy," also amplifying a tale from the Trojan War. Welcome!

With the retirement of Gwenyth Hood after twenty-two excellent years, new editors Victoria Gaydosik (fiction and general management) and Nolan Meditz (poetry) have introduced a few new ideas: for the first time, this issue includes audio files of each story and poem read by a cadre of volunteers on quite short notice. The files will be available at https://dc.swosu.edu/mcircle/. If this feature proves popular, we hope to repeat and expand it in next year's edition. Other plans include an index of every work published in *Mythril, Mythellany*, and *The Mythic Circle*; collections of individual writers' complete contributions as separate volumes where permitted; expanded graphic elements; celebratory volumes for our upcoming 50th anniversaries; and possible discussion forums through our archive on the Digital Commons. We hope to draw together the tradition of excellence behind us and add new digital features of interest to our readers. We welcome your insights and suggestions. → *Victoria Gaydosik, fiction editor and general manager*

From the Poetry Editor: I am Dr. Nolan Meditz, an Assistant Professor of Composition Studies at Southwestern Oklahoma State University, and it is my honor to serve as Poetry Editor for *The Mythic Circle*. For Issue 42, both Dr. Gaydosik and I have endeavored to compile the works that best exemplify mythic narrative and lyric composition.

In my role as poetry editor, I aim to select poems I feel leverage mythic tropes to speak to an innate sense of wonder about the world and/or retell old stories in interesting ways. I also try to find a balance of voices in the submissions I receive in order to reflect the variety of tales, contexts, and emotions that act as the foundation of mythopoeic literature. Individual poems in this volume achieve these editorial objectives by recontextualizing Homeric epics, providing stark images of ruined worlds, mourning the loss of magic, and singing to the beauty of ritual and nature, just to cite a few examples.

It is my hope that the poems you read here preserve the wonder, the mystery, and at times even the weirdness inherent to the mythopoeic.

Our Contributors

Kevan Kenneth Bowkett has been in the Canadian Reserves, washed dishes, planted trees, sold door-to-door, slept in an igloo, and run for Parliament. He's lectured at universities on the international arms trade, helped draft an International Convention on Evaluating New Technologies, and worked in a daycare. His play *Time's Fancy: The War of King Henry V and Joan of Arc* was shown at the Winnipeg Fringe Theatre Festival in 2017. His work has appeared in *Mythprint* and the *Manitoba Eco-Journal*, and he is currently working on a novel set in the fabled land of Cothirya.

Lawrence Buentello is a writer and poet living in San Antonio, Texas. A short story specialist, he has published innumerable tales in the fantasy, horror, and science fiction genres. He holds a traditional degree in English literature and has twenty-five years of experience working in academic libraries.

Joe R. Christopher has had one book of poems published by a standard publisher and a hundred or so individual poems in journals. He also has had over half a dozen books of other sorts appear from standard publishers, including a couple on C. S. Lewis. In his retirement, he is trying to turn some of the papers he read at meetings into publishable form-as well as writing more poems.

Janet Brennan Croft is a Reference Librarian at Rutgers University Libraries in New Jersey. She has written on J.R.R. Tolkien, Terry Pratchett, Lois McMaster Bujold, Joss Whedon, and other authors, TV shows, and movies, and is editor of many collections of literary essays, the most recent being *'Something Has Gone Crack': New Perspectives on Tolkien in the Great War* (Walking Tree, 2019). She edits the refereed scholarly journal *Mythlore*.

Holly Day's poetry has recently appeared in *Asimov's Science Fiction, Grain*, and *Harvard Review*. Her newest poetry collections are *Where We Went Wrong* (Clare Songbirds Publishing), *Into the Cracks* (Golden Antelope Press), *Cross Referencing a Book of Summer* (Silver Bow Publishing), and *The Tooth is the Largest Organ in the Human Body* (Anaphora Literary Press).

Mary Alice Dixon lives and writes in Charlotte, NC. She has a BA from Vassar College, an MA from Yale University, and a JD from Wake Forest University. Her recent writing is in, or forthcoming from, *Main Street Rag, Living Springs, Daniel Boone Footsteps, Stonecoast Review*, and elsewhere. You can often find her daydreaming about her childhood visits to her mother's family farm in West Virginia, where she first learned to talk with trees.

S. Dorman writes science fiction. Her essays have appeared in print publications such as *Extrapolation, An Unexpected Journal, Mythlore* and *Caleum et Terra*, and online in *Mere Orthodoxy* and *Superversive Inklings*. She writes allusive biblical fan fiction, satire, and rural town-in-transition Maine novels, holds an MA in humanities from California State University, Dominguez Hills, and has authored Maine creative nonfiction—*Maine Metaphor*—books published in series by Wipf & Stock.

Jillian Drinnon is an English Education major at Southwestern Oklahoma State University. She is also the rural reporter for The Gayly newspaper.

DC Mallery lives and writes in Southern California. His favorite quotation is from William Blake: "The road of excess leads to the palace of wisdom." Regrettably, he has neither been down that road nor entered that palace. Someday, he would like to hear colors, see sounds, and taste the flavors of words and numbers. A vast ocean of synesthesia awaits, if he could just find the door. This is his first story in *The Mythic Circle*. His debut novel—*Darksight*—was published in 2019. He can be found at <www.dcmallery.com>.

Mack W. Mani is an Oregon-based poet and author. In 2018 he was awarded Best Screenplay at the H.P. Lovecraft Film Festival. He currently co-hosts The Gentleman's Romantic Book Nook podcast.

Meg Moseman has been a fan of the Inklings since childhood. She presently lives in the mountains of Montana, where she puts her English degree to use in the children's section of an independent bookstore. In her spare time, she reads, writes, and illustrates fantasy and poetry. In addition to Lewis, Tolkien, and Williams, she loves Diana Wynne Jones, Kafka, Melville, Dickinson, and many others. Her poem "The Great Poet Emperor" appeared in *Heroic Fantasy Quarterly* in November 2017.

Dr. Brian Rickel deserves our thanks for figuring out how to get our pages properly numbered!

David Sparenberg is a ecosophic author and eco-poet, a staff member with OVI magazine, online from the EU. He presently has 4 e-books available in the OVI bookstore and has been honored to be an ongoing contributor to *INDIE SHAMAN* magazine in the UK over the past seven years. David also has 40+ videos viewable on YouTube. David lives in Seattle, WA.

Ella Wallsworth-Bell was brought up in a small village in Cornwall, in the far Southwest of England. She writes short stories that are modern takes on myth and magic, and which are strongly rooted in place and time. Themes include mental health in small communities, disability and acceptance, coping with motherhood, and escape, both physical and metaphorical. Cornwall has a rich heritage of myth, and our stories are often linked to the sea.

Amanda Weiss publishes under the name Ama Kirchner. She has stories in *Aliterate* and *Molotov Cocktail* and is a 2018 graduate of Clarion Workshop.

Kialey Varaksin is a student at Southwestern Oklahoma State University pursuing a degree in Environmental Science. In her free time, she enjoys being creative by drawing and painting.

Elizabeth Winterhalter goes by Athalie Genesis online. She has been practicing traditional art since the age of four and has been working digitally since 2011. She's had great fun learning more and more about life and art. She has worked professionally since 2014 and is looking for new ways to make others happy with her art. Her contact info is as follows: Instagram @Athalie_Genesis.

Lee Zumpe has been writing and publishing horror, dark fantasy and speculative fiction since the late 1990s. His short stories and poetry have appeared in a variety of publications such as *Weird Tales, Space and Time* and *Dark Wisdom*; and in anthologies such as *The Children of Gla'aki, Best New Zombie Tales* Vol. 3, *Through a Mythos Darkly, Heroes of Red Hook* and *World War Cthulhu*. His work has earned several honorable mentions in *The Year's Best Fantasy and Horror* collections. Lee is an entertainment editor for Tampa Bay Newspapers. Visit http://www.leeclarkzumpe.com.

Access the audio files identified by a speaker icon in each story and poem that follows at the Digital Archives of *The Mythic Circle* after August 1, 2021, at https://dc.swosu.edu/mcircle/ for free, or purchase a copy before then at http://www.mythsoc.org/mythic-circle.htm.

A Poem
by David Sparenberg

We Dreamed Ourselves Awake

One day we all woke up.
Every one of us really woke up.
We dreamed ourselves awake.

Nothing more
needed to be given
everything already
was given between us.

We all sat
at somebody else's table.
We all wore
somebody else's clothes.

Everyone inclusively
every one of us
drank from the life stream of creation.

Attentively
we dialogued together
in low tones
our voices soft and warm.

We understood
the bliss of love
the happy humility
of letting go.

We were awake!
Wakefulness
drummed in our kindred hearts
shone bravely
sweetly on our faces.

We looked
into one another
in the light of trust, blessed
with new eyes of renaissance.

We sat euphoric (drunk on presence)
in circles of others.
Peace was plentiful
within and between us. Earth
in the Dreaming rejoiced.

1

Falling for a Cornish Maid

by Ella Wallsworth-Bell

It's the girl's blue eyes that hook me in. She sits at the back of the pub, staring at me through a sea of cigarette smoke and a chatter of voices, incessant as waves on rocks. The Tinners Arms is packed on a Saturday night, when Zennor male voice choir meet up. Glasses chink and the punters pipe down to a reluctant hush. The publican folds pound notes into his palm for the drinks. We know the songs off by heart, mostly. All twenty voices together until I go for the solo. And the girl stares at me like she's worshipping the moon.

We do our favourite songs. "Sweet Nightingale." "Little Lize." "California Dreamin'," by the Mamas and Papas. And "Trelawney," of course. They sound like rugby anthems, rather than folk songs. Nearly all the lads in the choir are fishermen. And yet we rarely sing about fish, or the sea. The Beach Boys are the closest we get. Their harmonies whistle your soul, they do. We do a couple of modern tunes, like "A-ha." Anything except Abba. Too girly, they say.

We sing, and we drink, and I see the girl, with those beautiful eyes, glinting like rockpools trapped at the base of a cliff at low tide.

After choir finishes, I stay for another pint with my mate Jamie. He's buying, and I'm thirsty. "Who was that bird, over by the door?" I ask.

He frowns, like when I told him I was giving up fishing, to work the farm. "What you on about, Matt? Never saw no bird."

"Well, she were right there." I point with my pint-glass. "Lovely blue eyes she had and all."

He grins. "Missing out, am I? What was she wearing?" I try to think. "Can't quite remember."

Next week, darkness falls earlier. November is like that, in the far west of the county. Skies hang low, till they almost touch the cliff-tops. Dark sea, dark skies. All dark, by five o'clock. And the publican likes people to appreciate his roaring fire; he keeps the electric lights low, on purpose.

I stand tall and sing my heart out. It's the only time I fit into this group. I've got mud sticking to my boots instead of fish scales, like the others. One of the old boys wants the Scilly gig song, and I love the tune but hate the way it reminds me of the sea. Someone's got to work the family farm, and I'm the only one left. I scrape out a living on the rough and sandy soil of the cliff-tops, scratching away until I can raise a crop, or feed a raggedy flock of sheep, or simply until the bare-faced crows rip into the freshly ploughed field to rob the seeds before they sprout. Farming's tough, in west Cornwall. I gave up my boat for it, and I wish I hadn't.

Tonight, when the song ends, I open my eyes and see that girl again, staring right at me. Cold, fresh salt-filled air rushes over from her, as if I'm standing on a beach in a storm. I breathe in deep, to refresh my lungs. A tear rolls down her pale, smooth cheeks. She lets it slide, and it wets a curl of ice-blonde hair. Her waist and legs are hidden behind the people sitting at the table in front of her. I shift myself, trying to keep sight of her, but then I see her chair is empty. She's gone.

"See'd her again, 'ave 'ee?" Jamie asks, his face weathered and windburned. "Gone a'ready?" He passes me a pint and I slurp it. "Tell you what, mate, I'll go over and show you where she were sitting."

We both walk over to the door and I point out the seat. It's ancient, and I run my hands over the twists and turns in the carved teak.

"Alright." He pauses, looks at the floor. "Well, she spilt her pint." I look down at a puddle of liquid on the stone slabs. Weird—I never saw a drink in her hand. I think—though again, I'm not sure—she had her hands folded in her lap.

Jamie puts his hand on the shoulder of the man on the next table. I can't hear what he's saying, but he guffaws, and the old boy bangs his stick on the floor. Vibrations pulse through the thick soles of my boots.

He turns back to face me. "Reckon you've got no belly for the booze these days, Matt me man. That were a youngster from the packing sheds, over St Ives way."

"Really?" I can't imagine her picking crabmeat.

"Need to get yer eyes tested, mate. Weren't no bird you were geeking at. He's a bloke, ain't he?" He laughs.

I pull a face. "No, no you've got it wrong. A girl she was. Honest to God."

Another week passes, and it's choir-night again. This time, I nudge Jamie when I see her. Suddenly, she's sitting there, on that ancient chair, staring at me. There's a half-smile on her lips, red as fronds of rich velvet seaweed. I start my solo and her eyes shine.

Jamie glances over and shakes his head at me. After the song, I rush over to talk to her. I want to find out who she is, and how she's got the whole pub believing she's some gypsy lad.

But I find myself, half a pint sloshing in my glass, standing alone at the door by her empty chair.

I curse, shaking my head. All I want to know is who she is. And find out why she's noticed me. I'm looking forward to coming here every week to see her. God knows I've nothing else to stare at all week, with my head down in the stony fields.

"Dunno what you're on about." Jamie's voice, behind me. "I saw him. Sat right on this chair. Definitely one of they gypsies."

I slam my glass down on the nearest table.

"Summat weird here, though." He leans down, crouches at the foot of the chair.

"That there." He holds up his fingertip. I see a small, shiny, translucent disc. "Fish-scale, see? That stranger's a fisherman, I reckon. But not from round here."

I walk out the door.

I don't follow the thick rutted track homeward, under the stars, to a lonely farm-house smelling of damp, and clagged with mud.

I turn downhill, heading for the cliffs. I breathe in great lungfuls of sea air. I taste salt when I lick my lips. My heart thuds in my chest when I see her. Not two hundred yards away from me, she stands silhouetted against the star-gazy sky. Bracken catches against my trouser legs.

She stands on the cliff path, her fair hair falling across her face.

"Who are you?" I ask. "Where you from? And why'd you disappear off so quick?" I reach out, and softly brush a curl from her cheeks.

"I like the sound of your voice. And the look of you, too." Her voice is quiet, like the trickle of a stream toppling into the sea from a great height. Her chin is square, her shoulders firm and strong. Is she a woman, a man, or a sea-witch? I don't care, and I kiss her. She smells of hot sand on a summer day, and I close my eyes. I've no idea how I get home, or how much of the night is lost.

From that first night on, she's all I can think of. I sit, back against the stone wall, and stare out from the top field. The surface of the sea glitters intoxicatingly; I imagine how refreshing cold it would be, deep below. Closing my eyes at night, I hear a rushing in my ears, as if the sea is calling to me. I'm not only falling in love, but drowning in it.

On choir night, Jamie has a word with me. We stand face to face across the hard wooden table, legs apart and voices blazing.

"What you playing at?" His face reddens. "Everyone's talking. You're carrying on with a, a," he hisses at me, sharp as a wounded conger eel, "boy."

I raise my voice, argue back. "You haven't seen her, not properly. She listens to me."

"So do I. For too damn long."

There's a ringing in my ears, as if a hurricane is howling off Land's End. "She's strange, and beautiful, and she reminds me of the sea."

I storm out the pub, slamming the door behind me. I rush down to the cliff path. She's there to meet me, and I hold her tight. She whispers in my ear of deepwater and moonlight. I breathe in, not caring if she switches between male and female, human and sea-creature. I slip my hands down to her waist and am not surprised when I feel the smooth skid of scales under my fingers.

"Take me with you," I say.

She smiles. "Come with me, Mathew Trewhela with the beautiful voice. Come with me, and sing to our children, under the sea." She walks to the cliff-edge. It's a two hundred foot sheer drop to the still, dark ocean.

I gulp, shivering with cold.

And, wrapped in her silken strong embrace, we jump. Air rushes past my ears and she tells me not to be afraid. I've never been happier. I'm with her, and I'm free to be me.

Bird w/ Flowers by Kialey Varaksin

Betrothal

by Lawrence Buentello

Grayson first saw her as she rode from the trees of the forest beyond his small house. The sun, with the last of the light it threw over the hills to the west, illuminated her astride her horse in burnished gold and yellow streaks. But even as the sun set, she glowed, and her horse also shone with a pure white light that brightened the long grasses over which she rode. She paced her horse before his small house in the country, while he stood leaning against the wood posts of the corral in which his own mare nervously stirred.

With every pass she came nearer, and when she was near enough, even as the darkness of the evening swept over the fields, he clearly saw her face, which was beautiful and perfect, and her long, white hair, which contrasted strangely with her youth. The fierce red eyes of her mount told him that neither was moving in a body of flesh, but that they were composed of a spiritual fabric that left no sound as the horse trampled the field. She bade to him with a thin, white hand, and called his name repeatedly, *Grayson, O Grayson, come to me, my love—*

But the young man only bent to lift the lantern at his feet, and sparked his tinder to light it in a familiar way. He raised the lantern as high as his shoulder and watched her ride, hoping the light would turn her away. She and the horse stood still after a while, her diaphanous gown billowing in a nonexistent breeze, her hair rising on a supernatural wind, her lips parted, but not moving, as she said, *Grayson, O Grayson, come to me, my love—*

No! he shouted, *I will not come with you! Go away!*

But she wouldn't go away, no matter how many times he implored her to leave, nor did the horse move from where it stood.

He turned, following the halo of light cast from the lantern as he carried it into the small house. He shut the door and windows, despite the warmth of the evening. From time to time he peered from behind the shutters to see her waiting in the field beyond the house, glowing like the dying embers of a fire, before turning away from the sight of her and struggling to find sleep. He slept alone, since his mother, father, and brother had died of the same fever that left him untouched. In this house of death, he was alive, but haunted by the dead, and now *she* had come back to him. He knew her presence was unnatural—he'd dreamt of her many times over the previous week, perhaps presaging her actual appearance—but the apparition beyond the house wasn't her, only a *ghost* of her, shining like the moon.

Grayson visited the priest's house the next day.

The old man was a humble man, having served the people of the village for many years, through fevers and plagues, without once having been touched by sickness. This gave him a reputation as one allied with divine grace, though the priest never asked for more in tithing from the villagers than he needed to survive.

So Grayson traveled long miles from his father's farm to receive a blessing.

"Why do you wish to be blessed?" the priest asked as he met Grayson beneath the sun. His clouded blue eyes shone behind pale wrinkles. "Are you ill?"

"No, Father," Grayson said, glancing back nervously to where his mare stood tied to a post. He met the old man's gaze again, still trying to find the right words to describe his problem. "I am being haunted."

The priest raised his white eyebrows. "Haunted? Where? At your father's house?"

"It's not the house, Father. *I* am being haunted."

"By what?"

"By the ghost of Heather Wade."

The old priest studied Grayson's face a moment, then nodded. "Come into my house and explain yourself, young Grayson."

Grayson sat with the priest at his table, recounting his courtship of Heather, and their family's mutual acceptance of a possible betrothal. This the priest already knew, for he made it his business to know the matrimonial intentions of his people. But before their bond could deepen, and be consecrated by the priest, Heather and her family had succumbed to the same fever that claimed Grayson's family, too.

Though Grayson had felt a growing affection for the girl, he could not say that he loved her, though he was greatly saddened by her death.

But now she had returned from the place of the dead, manifesting before his house, entreating him to join her; now he feared for his life, and the blackening of his soul if he were to cavort with spirits.

"This is very serious," the old man said. "Are you certain what you've seen is real? Have you been drinking ale or wine?"

"No, Father," Grayson said. He recalled her waiting on her horse in the twilight of the day and shuddered. "You may follow me home if you wish to see for yourself."

The priest sat back in his chair. "I believe you have seen something terrifying to you, son. Whether it be the spirit of Heather Wade or not, I couldn't say. I blessed the graves of the girl and her family, so how could she rise as a spirit?"

"I don't know," Grayson said, knowing that he was speaking a lie.

"If it were truly the ghost of Heather, then something profound must have motivated her shade to return to you. Tell me truthfully—were you betrothed?"

Grayson bowed his head, ashamed of his deception. "No, Father. Had we been betrothed, you would have consecrated our union."

When Grayson looked up again into the priest's eyes, he hoped his lie wasn't writ across his face.

"Very well," the old man said. "Then something else is plaguing you, perhaps some demonic imp that has nothing to do with Heather Wade. You are living alone now, Grayson, and men who live alone often find themselves the prey of supernatural temptations. Guard against any consorting with devilry."

The old priest blessed Grayson that day, praying sincerely for the boy's protection. But all the while the boy listened to the old man's Latin utterances, he felt guilt for his sin. He'd lied to the priest, but had he really lied? Heather had orchestrated their meeting with the hermit of the woods, and Grayson had only placated her wishes because he wanted to be with her sensually. But the hermit held no divine powers, surely, not like the priest.

After receiving the old man's blessing, Grayson thanked him with the few pennies in his possession, mounted his horse, and rode back to his father's farm.

§

She returned that night, despite the priest's blessing, her horse capering on the field beyond the house, calling—*Grayson, come with me, my love! You are my betrothed, pledged to be with me!*

He stood with his fingers pressed into the wood of the window sill, staring at the phantasm moving gracefully beneath the light of the half moon. Though he prayed, he knew his prayers would not be heard. He'd lied to the priest, and so his sin was being repaid with indifference.

I will not go to you, I won't!

Grayson shuttered the window and sat by the small fire of the hearth, rocking slowly on his knees, wondering what he could possibly do to send her spirit away.

Yes, she loved him. He knew this to be true. But he didn't love her, nor even wanted her, beyond that night—

Before the fever had swept through the countryside, while they were both still healthy and young, he pursued Heather Wade with a sensual desire that would not be denied. Yet she denied him, while professing love for him. Neither his father nor hers would allow the priest to betroth them so impetuously, though she begged her father on many occasions. Without a proper betrothal, which she insisted would bond them together forever, in this life and the next, she wouldn't allow him to lie with her, which he desperately desired.

8

There seemed no solution to their dilemma, until she spoke of the old hermit of the hills.

Heather had been a wild girl in many ways. She'd believed in the old wives' tales of gathering magic from the plants and the trees, and of heathen practitioners who still embraced the dark arts. Her mother had told her of the old hermit in the hills, who had once been a man in their village, but whose insistence on practicing forbidden magic forced the priest to exile him to the wilderness.

Certainly, for a few pennies, the old hermit would bind them with his arts; they would be forever betrothed, and able to consummate their love without sin.

Grayson didn't believe in magical hermits and would have laughed at her silliness if he hadn't desired her so much.

So they set out one morning, walking into the hills until they *did* find an old man living in the woods who claimed to be a sorcerer (among many absurd mantles). This old man, Seamus of the Hills, laughed through his long, white beard, accepted their pennies, and chanted before a small fire set burning amongst the trees. He took Heather's hand in his left hand, and Grayson's in his right, and pressed them together as he sang in an unknown language.

After the final note of his song, he declared the boy and girl now bonded, betrothed in this world and the divine, never to be separated by life or death.

That night, after they returned to the village, she lay with him and he was finally satisfied, but it was only a sensual desire he fulfilled, for he felt no love for her.

Neither his parents nor hers ever discovered their "betrothal," and now they all were dead, except for Grayson, and the spirit on a ghostly horse that pranced beyond his house in the dark of the frightening world.

He did not sleep that night. On the morrow, he would seek out the old hermit again, the priest's blessing having failed in its intended purpose, and beg him to use his magic to send her away.

§

The next morning, Grayson commenced on foot through the hills, having left his horse corralled since the beast would move only with difficulty over the rocky falls and rises. When they earlier journeyed through the hills in search of the old man, Heather seemed to know which way to move from rise to rise, as if she'd traveled there before; now Grayson felt lost in the tendrils of fog caressing the grass, so that after a pair of hours, the sun failing to chase the clouds from the hills, he began calling out for the old man, Seamus, more frantically with every passing minute.

As Grayson sat on a large stone gathering his wits, he lowered his head in prayer a moment, then raised his eyes to see the old man penetrating the fog like a ghost walking across the vale.

The hermit laughed and spiked his walking staff before the young man's feet. "Pray not for holy intervention into unholy things."

Grayson stood, unnerved by the hermit's sudden appearance. "I've come into the hills to seek your guidance."

"Why else would you appear before me?" The old man touched his white hair thoughtfully, a terrible smile rising in his beard. "I see the lust is gone from your eyes, as it enthralled you at your last visit. Replaced by something less enchanted, I perceive. Where is the lass to whom I bound you in betrothal? Has she left you for another?"

"She is dead."

"Then let us mourn for her soul. Or would you have me mourn?"

Within the intrusive fingers of fog, Grayson recounted his Heather's death, her arrival as a specter, and his deception of the priest. And, most of all, he emphasized his great desire to be free of her supernatural beseeching of his love, of which he had none to give her, if he ever loved her in life.

"There must be a way to break this betrothal," Grayson implored the old man of the hills. "You who bound us must be able to break that bond as well. Surely there must be a way?"

Seamus cackled wickedly, his laugh echoing through the shrouded hills. He stamped his staff into the ground repeatedly, as if enjoying, beyond measure, the young man's dilemma, before leaving it standing in the ground of its own powers. "Then you admit you did not love the girl?"

Grayson shook his head ashamedly. "No."

"You merely wanted to satisfy your carnal needs, and now you wish release from the shade that loves you still?"

"Yes, I confess this to you! Judge me if you will, but free me from her torment!"

"Her love is a torment to you?"

"She wishes me to die to satisfy her love. And I do not wish to die."

"Yes, I see the fear in your eyes. How sad it is to see a man, even a young man, fear such a powerful act of love. But so be it."

The old hermit reached into his filthy vestments and retrieved a small wooden vial capped with moss. "Drop this powder into water and drink it before you sleep. Thereafter you shall meet your betrothed in your dreams so you may confess to her that you don't truly love her. No harm will come to your body, such as a spirit might render unto flesh, for dreams are ethereal. Your confession will set you free."

Grayson accepted the vial, but shook his head. "I do not wish to confront her again, even in my dreams."

"Only your confession will make you free of her inveigling spirit."

The young man gazed at the vial in his fingers, terrified of confronting Heather in his reveries. "I have no pennies to trade you."

The hermit only laughed at this admission of poverty, pulled his staff from the earth, then turned away and began walking back through the fog. He said, as he disappeared into the fog, "In sleep you'll find your freedom. Sleep well, young fool."

§

She continued haunting his nights as he shuttered his father's house and tried to sleep amidst her plaintive calls for him, and though he now possessed the ability to confront her through the dark gifts of the hermit, he couldn't bring himself to consume the powder.

Night after night, Grayson sat cross-legged by the fire of the hearth, listening to her unearthly voice, tending the terrible guilt he carried for having deceived her in life. What could he possibly say to her in death that would cause her to forgive him?

Night after night he heard her weeping on the wind, her separation from him an unbearable sorrow that ached in her voice.

Grayson endured her cries as long as possible, until one night he simply couldn't stand hearing her moans penetrate the shutters of the house any longer, and resolved to finally face her in his dreams. He tapped the contents of the wooden vial into a cup of old ale, stirring the powder into the liquid with the vial in which it came. Then, girding his courage as a man might heel a horse through treacherous terrain, he drank the ale and dropped the cup onto the floor. Thereafter, not knowing what to expect from the old hermit's enchantment, he lay by the guttering fire of the hearth and closed his eyes.

When once again he became aware of the world, he was standing in a vast meadow trimmed in shimmering grass and foxtail, the land beneath glowing supernaturally, as if it were consumed by mist. He realized that he must be dreaming, but the fidelity of this dream was unlike any he'd ever experienced. He stood searching for the sun, but the sky shone as a uniform blue swath as dense as the surface of a pool.

Was this vision the effect of the powder he'd consumed? And wasn't he meant to confront his lost betrothed in his dream?

Grayson had little time to consider these questions, for in a moment she appeared, walking toward him from the hills, but not spectrally—the girl who stood before him was his own Heather Wade as she appeared in life, her tawny hair lifted by an unfelt wind, her green eyes glistening in the sunless light. Great happiness shone in her face, her smile radiant and warm, as it always shone when he kissed her in the meadows by her family's farm.

"Grayson, my love!" she said. "I knew you'd come to me!"

He moved toward her, now unafraid of her presence, since she no longer wore white hair and deathly pale flesh. He reached out his hand to her, and she reached out her hand to his, but neither felt the touch of the other.

"Why can't I feel your hand?" she asked, sorrow coming into her eyes.

Grayson stood confounded by her beauty, struck by the same desire he'd felt for her before her death—at last he found the words to speak as he moved his hand away.

"We're meeting only in a dream," he said. "The old hermit of the hills gave me a powder to meet you in this way so I could tell you what I must. Heather, you must go away from me."

"Grayson, why do you say this?" She reached to embrace him, but could not transgress the limitations of his dream. "You must come with me and be with me forever. We are betrothed!"

"You died from a fever, my Heather. And I survived and walk among the living still. You must cease trying to take me away with you, for I still have a long life to live on earth."

"No! We swore before the hermit that we would stay together, forsaking all things. Even if I died, our souls must stay bonded throughout eternity!"

"We cannot, poor Heather."

"We must! Grayson, don't you love me?"

He stared into her pretty face, his heart flooded by guilt for abusing her trust in life. But he remembered the long nights listening to the haunted beseeching of her ghost, and the fear her spectral visage left within him, and knew he must rid himself of her presence forever.

"I never loved you, Heather," he said, watching the anguish press deep lines into her mouth and cheeks. "I lied to you because I desired you. I was foolish, and sinful, for stealing your affection only to satisfy myself, but that is the truth and I am sorry. But you must go away from me now and be among the dead."

"I don't believe you," she said, shaking her head. "Seamus consecrated our betrothal;` you swore a vow among the hills. You are bound to me!"

"No, Heather. Our union wasn't sanctioned by the priest, only presided over by some mad heathen of the forest. We were never bonded, nor did I ever love you. I have a life to live now, I must marry and have children to work my family's farm with me. And you must go on."

"You would marry another? But you swore your love for me—"

"I lied to you, Heather! Now go away from me! I never loved you."

He'd never seen such sorrow as that expressed upon the young girl's face, the wide eyes and withered lips—without another word she turned away from him and began walking back through the meadow, her sobbing nothing less but the most melancholy music he'd ever heard, further and further away from him until she vanished into the glimmering grass and he was alone, all alone, in his dream.

§

Heather Wade's phantasm never returned to Grayson after that night, though for many evenings he stood by the old corral waiting for her to appear. He wished to apologize to her once again, for the guilt he carried with him felt like a dozen sacks of grain upon his back. The memory of her weeping in his dream as she left him forever, the dimensions of her heartbreak, were so vast that he felt the pain of it within his own heart, a pain which plagued him all of his years.

The guilt of his sin weighed so heavily on his conscience that he could never marry or father children; he knew that when he died no one would remain to carry on the traditions of his family.

In the years before his death he spent much time searching for the old hermit to give him some new powder to alleviate his guilt, but the old man had vanished with the fog.

§

When Grayson died, alone in a cold, dark room, he remained alone in death, betrothed only to the memory of his sins which, in his old age, seemed no less heavy than a great, abiding love.

Untitled by Kialey Varaksin

What Iphigenia Knows

by Ama Kirchner

1. Iphigenia is in a void. The space surrounding her is not black or gray, nor is it faded light that tapers off at the edges of her vision. It is the absence of light, of sound, of temperature, time and space. Iphigenia's universe begins and ends with the contours of her body: the span of her wings, the tips of her outstretched claws. Her snout. She flexes her talons and marvels as they retract slowly into her scaly flesh. Her body was different before. Wasn't it?

2. Yes. Smooth tan skin, dark curled hair, a splayed-out scar on her knee from falling from an olive tree as a child. She remembers the fall, how her brother cried out "Iphigenia, Iphigenia," a bleating sound that made her laugh through the tears because he sounded like one of their goats. She remembers her mother's hands descending from the sky, then rising towards her mother's bosom like she was flying home.

3. Iphigenia knows she is dead.

Bronze refracted light across her face, a thousand helmets blazing in the noonday sun. Beneath them, a thousand smiles. She could smell sea salt, feel the light reflecting off the waves. Teeth. So many teeth, all lined in a row, like little white soldiers.

4. The screaming wakes her up. It hisses at first, like an ocean being boiled away to nothing, and later, it roars. There is now a solidness akin to ground beneath her. Iphigenia stands tentatively on shaky feet, struggling to balance with her body's new dimensions. Her wings are heavy. They drag behind her as she wanders in the direction of the sound, limping, her talons clicking as they meet floor.

The sounds change as she wanders. At times it is a hissing sizzle, the sound of fat on a hot stone. Other times it sounds like the moment when lighting strikes a tree and a limb falls off with a great crack. And at times it sounds like the bellow of the wind filling a great ship's sails. Iphigenia wanders, following the trail of sounds until she comes across three women, their dog-faces stained in offal. They look like her—or she like them. Sisters.

"There you are," hisses the eldest, tall and black with fire for eyes.

"Eat up, little one," hisses the middle one, motioning her closer with a soft leather wing.

The youngest one simply snarls, tarry ichor dripping from her fangs.

14

The three women stand upon a colossal body suspended in empty space, a body like a planet. A titan. A river of tears flows in torrents from the titan's eyes as the youngest suddenly rips into his belly, crowing with pleasure. Iphigenia's nostrils flare. She is hungry.

Iphigenia looks at the titan and the titan looks at her. In his eyes she sees two earths, one superimposed over the other. The first is primordial and raw, fecund with life. Strange creatures populate the earth. The second is ancient and dying, the earth burned raw by a dying sun. She watches as the stars blink in and out of existence and the world is made and unmade. She watches gods at war, men at war, a girl on a ship, her auburn hair braided in gold thread. A ring glints on her finger.

"Ignore him," hisses the middle sister.

Iphigenia watches as the image of the girl is replaced by her own reflection, a monstress with wet eyes red as cinnabar. Her thin wings are folded around herself like a threadbare blanket. She looks small. Her image fades and the titan looks at her, and in his eyes, she sees pity.

Iphigenia's stomach lurches. She shrieks, ripping into the titan's body in a frenzy. Her teeth slice through the skin and muscle neatly. She is surprised to find the taste of ichor as sweet as honey-wine.

5. Her mother had a copper mirror, shined to a gloss. "These barbarians like to be pale," she said with a backward glance, applying a white powder until her golden face lost its boldness and shine. Her mother's features were rare. How proud her father must have been when he returned with her from the war.

"Let me try!" cried her brother, his little hands scrambling for the powder. Iphigenia laughed as her mother dabbed a small dot of white on the end of his nose. He was a striking child, soft brown curls that turned gold in the sun.

Iphigenia tousled her brother's hair as she slid into the place beside her mother. She looked at her mother's profile, the curve of her neck, the line of glowing skin at the edge of her hairline where she had yet to apply the mercury. The line of gold that was her true mother. She wished she could take a cloth and wipe it all off.

"Your betrothed has sent you a ring," said her mother, taking Iphigenia's hand. "Remember. A ring is a promise."

The ring was hammered gold and topaz, a beautiful but imperfect circle. It felt cold against her skin.

6. She awakens with a gasp, her body entangled with the three sisters. They lie intertwined in a nest on the titan. His chest moves up and down, the slow movement of a ship cresting a gentle wave. Iphigenia looks downwards to see his entrails, to find the wounds she has inflicted, but the flesh is already pink and healing. She looks up and sees the titan is staring at her.

"I'm sorry," she hisses, ashamed.

The titan continues to stare. In his eyes, astrolabes exist alongside starships. In his eyes, Troy is yet to be built, and Troy has already fallen.

"DEATH WILL BE MY WEDDING," says the titan king, unblinking, and Iphigenia flinches as if she has been slapped.

7. "I named you Iphigenia," said her mother. "Because it means strong or stout. A woman must be strong to survive in this world." Iphigenia drew a comb through her mother's hair. The breeze was soft upon her face, the olive grove bathed in dappled light.

"And what does my name mean, Momma?" her brother asked. He sat cross-legged beside her, a game of knucklebones in his lap.

"He who would conquer mountains," said her mother, smiling. She leaned forward to kiss him on the forehead. "Though for now, you're still a little mountain."

Her brother made a face. "I want to conquer mountains."

"Then first you'll have to conquer me in a game of knucklebones," laughed Iphigenia, opening her eyes. She took one from his little hand and tossed it high in the air, watching as it rolled, sharp white against the cerulean sky.

8. Iphigenia bears witness to the punishments.

Through the titan's eyes, she sees the eldest sister disembowel a young boy who hid an asp in his father's bed, a talon thrust through his chest and out the other side. She watches the middle sister remove the head of an unfaithful wife, pausing to lick bloody tissue hanging like wet lace. The youngest shrieks before a hiccupping child who danced in a god's sacred grove, delighting as blood trickles from his ears in thin rivulets. Iphigenia turns away in disgust.

"Why do they punish?" she asks the titan. His eyes are galaxies now, limitless and unfathomable. She shivers, pulling her wings in around herself. "What was your crime?" she whispers.

Iphigenia is not surprised when he does not answer.

9. The wind slapped against her face, beat it. Through bleary eyes she saw her mother's beautiful mercury-painted face shining from the dock. She was shouting, but Iphigenia couldn't hear anything over the creaking of the ship, the flapping sails.

"What is it?" cried Iphigenia, her face wet with ocean spray. Her mother called again, but each time the wind rose to match her volume.

"Mother, I can't hear you!" she cried, increasingly desperate.

Something glinted at the periphery of her vision and Iphigenia looked down, noticing the ring as if for the first time. When she looked up again the coast was far away. Her mother was gone.

10. Today the titan is a wintry lake, a soft grey fog rolling across his surface. Iphigenia lies on a rocky outpost at his center watching the punishments in the water. The girl has narrow shoulders. She is hiding behind an outcrop of rocks along the beach, her breath emerging in little gasps. The limestone cliff is a white slash of stone above, the sea a lapis lazuli blue. Iphigenia can see little freckles on her nose, uneven and brown, and a small dot of green at the middle of her brown eyes. This girl could be her sister. Could have been.

"What is her crime?" asks Iphigenia. The sisters alight, their talons clicking on the pebbled shore as they approach.

PATRICIDE, booms the titan.

The youngest sister leaps forward, scoring a shallow strike along the girl's upper arm. She crows with pleasure as the blood arcs like a rainbow into the yellow soil.

"Why did she do it?" asks Iphigenia. The girl is howling now, her mouth a round O, the whites of her eyes flashing. Iphigenia is glad she cannot hear her.

FOR HIS CRIMES AGAINST HER.

The middle sister shrieks and the girl doubles over, her hands clasped tight against her ears. Blood pours between her hands. The eldest approaches.

"How do we punish those who kill their daughters?" asks Iphigenia, her throat tight. The titan pauses.

WE DO NOT.

With a quick thrust of her foot, the eldest sister slits the girl's throat. She collapses in a heap on the beach. They stand over her still form, three massive black silhouettes on a white beach.

The image dissolves and Iphigenia looks at her reflection in the water, the acid red eyes, the black and scaly hide. There is a pain, a thrumming in her chest; she hears the sound of wind against a ship's sails. With a shriek Iphigenia slashes her talon through the water, her image destroyed. Ripples within ripples drift to the edges of the lake.

BUT MOTHERS WILL.

11. Iphigenia's mother:

> • liked to trace Iphigenia's nose at night when she pretended to be asleep, but they both knew that Iphigenia was awake. She often told Iphigenia that she looked just

like her grandfather, the one she would never meet. "Did he die in the war?" Iphigenia asks, but what she wants to ask is: was Father the one who killed him? Her mother's mouth draws into a line and that is the only answer she will ever receive.

• called her brother "my heart," and Iphigenia, "my soul."

• watched the sea every morning, her eyes hungry for home.

• ate olives all the time. She told Iphigenia that the olives from her country were darker, saltier, better. That she loved honey as a child but now all she wanted was the taste of salt. Iphigenia made a face. "Impossible! That will never happen to me!" And it doesn't, because she never becomes a woman.

12. "I have a mother," says Iphigenia. "A home." Her sisters look at her, their serpent tongues flicking, their nictitating eyes blinking slowly. They watch as her wings unfurl. She tests them experimentally, once, twice. What will her mother think of her new body—the talons, the fangs? How much time has passed? Iphigenia does not care. She pushes off with her powerful legs and finds it easier than expected, the titan's colossal body now twinkling far below her like a distant star.

13. There is the sound of beating winds and then the world is suddenly bright and glistening. It is loud. The sky shines blue and pale, the vault of heaven rises far above. Seagulls fly abreast of her and the taste of salt rings on her lips. There are so many smells here, so many sensations. She can feel time advancing, the parameters of space. She can feel the wind.

She follows it like a thread, slowly moving in the direction of her mother. Her senses are sharper than anything she has experienced before, the smells almost an assault after the austerity of the void. How can humans bear the salt, the moisture, the press of sand and ocean spray and dust upon their skin? How can they bear all this light, this detail? She flies quickly, and there, sees the place where her ship disembarked, there, the wooden dock where she saw her mother for the last time. In the distance stands a palace, she knows, and beyond that, the grove. Her mother is in the grove. Her heart beats like war drums as her wings carry her home.

The grove is the same as she remembered it. Brown-green grass and squat olive trees, small rucksacks here and there from olive pickers. She closes her wings around herself, tries to make herself look smaller, less monstrous. She is embarrassed by what she has become. And yet her heart rises as she follows the thread to the center of the grove.

There. A mound of earth, hastily covered. A grave with no marker, not a proper burial for anyone, especially a queen. Iphigenia holds her face to her hands and falls to the earth. The smell of the soil is more final, even, than the darkness of the void.

14. Bronze glints in the sunlight. Sails fill with wind. A girl screams. Iphigenia remembers.

15. *The harbor was filled to the edges with warships, sails upon sails stacked against the gray horizon. None of the sails were moving. All was still, as if the wind had deposited her where she was to go and just as*

quickly died, its mission complete. The slaves bent over their oars, exhausted, their backs gleaming with sweat and blood.

She searched for her betrothed on the approaching dock, her eyes scanning for the hero out of legend, and instead she found her father. Tall, proud, broad. His armor reflected the sun back at her. She held her hand up to cover her eyes.

"Father," she said, as she walked down the gangplank flanked by the soldiers. She leaned forward to kiss him and he leaned away, his eyes averted.

So this is war, the girl thought.

16. *They led her, trembling, to the wedding altar. She wore white, gold threads woven throughout her hair as her mother taught her. Legions of her father's men stood from side to side in their best uniforms, armor polished and blinding. These were men who could conquer mountains. So much sun and so little wind. The harbor was far too still.*

She walked up to the altar, her eyes cast down and away from her husband to be, the demi-god rumored to be beautiful as the sun. She searched instead for her father's gaze, but his eyes were on the sea. His profile was different with the helmet. He looked like a statue.

"Father?" said Iphigenia.

Her father lunged forward, grabbing her braid with one hand. Iphigenia shrieked at the pain as her head was yanked sideways, her thin back striking the hard wood of the altar with a crack. She could see the sky above darkening.

"Father!" screamed Iphigenia, twisting sideways. "Why are you doing this?" She saw her betrothed, the great hero, grimly press something shining into her father's hand. The hands that had lifted her up to toss her towards the sky, the hands that had played with her auburn hair. The edges of Father's mouth were downturned. There was grey in his beard that she had never seen before.

"Why?" cried Iphigenia. Her father's face was a twisted mask. He pushed her head away, towards the watching men of her father's fleet, the ships in the still harbor. Her heart was bursting through her ribcage.

A seagull swooped over the troops. There was a flash of light and a sharp pain as something plunged into her chest. Pain. Everywhere, pain. A breeze caressed her skin. The men murmured. The breeze grew in strength, blowing harder and harder until it became a wind. The pain in her chest began to fade. The men erupted in cheers but the sound was distant now, muffled. As the world receded she could hear the men chanting to the rhythm of the war drums.

"Onward to Troy! Onward to victory!"

17. "Iphigenia!" says her mother, turning.

They are standing on a ship, the same ship that took her to her death. Her mother wears her favorite dress, a simple linen chiton the color of dried grass. There is a cup of honey-wine in her hand. "Iphigenia," she says again, smiling. "I've been waiting for you."

They are alone. No wind pulls at the ship. The light is flat and bright. Iphigenia moves closer.

"Mother?" she hisses. She tries to keep her mouth closed, ashamed of her rust-colored fangs, her cinnabar eyes. She pulls her wings in tight around herself.

"Sit here, child," says her mother, her eyes warm. "Let me have a look at you." She beckons Iphigenia to her side. As Iphigenia approaches she sees there is a slash of red at her mother's neck, dried blood at the edges. Iphigenia's face is hot. "Who did this to you?" she asks.

"Come now, sit child," says her mother. She sits on a wooden bench and holds her hand out to Iphigenia, who sits beside her.

"Do not look at me," says Iphigenia.

"My soul," says her mother, stroking her scales. "How beautiful you are." She smiles, taking Iphigenia's talons into her hands. Her teeth are stained red.

"Did you kill Father?" asks Iphigenia.

"Of course," her mother says. She takes a sip of honey-wine, her eyes hard.

"And who killed you?" asks Iphigenia. "A soldier? A god?" She swallows. "Was it my sisters?"

"Does it matter?" says her mother, stroking Iphigenia's cheek, her eyes soft now. "It's all over now." Iphigenia looks at her mother's throat, the inside of her neck exposed. She sees a glint of white bone and has to choke back the rising bile.

"Why don't the gods avenge the daughters?" asks Iphigenia, hot ichor pumping in her veins. Her eyes are burning but she does not cry.

Her mother's eyes never leave Iphigenia's face. "Perhaps because they know that mothers always will."

They sit there, the boat rolling slowly on the placid sea, for a long time. Iphigenia traces her mother's face—the smile lines, the scar on her chin, the crow's nest at the corner of her eyes. The sky darkens and her mother gradually fades like mist into the starless night.

18. Iphigenia awakens in the grove, her face buried in the soil of her mother's grave. The air is still, though there remains a soft scent of lavender. Her mother's favorite oil. She sees soft brown curls and a laughing face over a game of knucklebones. Iphigenia opens her eyes to

look up to find her sisters perched in the trees around her. "Come now, sister," hisses the eldest. "It is time to go home."

"No," says Iphigenia. "Not yet."

19. Iphigenia descends in the skies over Argos, the buildings small and white against a blue so uniform in color that sky is sea and sea is sky. There is running, screaming. Doors slam shut as she approaches, a collective sigh that becomes a groan and then a tremor. "Erinyes!" calls one voice, and then another, and then it becomes a mantra, a chant of dread welcoming her and her sisters.

She alights at the top of the temple and takes in the view. Cypress trees stand here and there in solitude against the sky, from a distance resembling a man or god in wait. This land of soft rolling hills and olive trees, of lemon and fig-scent. Her home.

"Iphigenia, please..." she hears a whisper on the wind. It sounds like her mother.

Her sisters swoop and shriek, leering at running crowds below. They are beautiful. Their steel-sharp talons dried with rust, their black wings thin and slippery and dark as the night. She whistles to them and they turn in formation, their collective gaze focused, coral-sharp, on their prey.

The boy is running for a nearby grove. This boy, Iphigenia recalls, was once her brother.

20. Perhaps in time they could let the titan go free. No punishment should be eternal, after all, even as unspeakable a crime as matricide. Iphigenia figured that a long time ago.

Perhaps, too, she can eventually forgive her father, the soldiers, her former husband-to-be. Those hands that took her life for a war. Those hands that sent her hurtling into the void. Perhaps she can forgive her brother, too.

Today is not that day.

She breathes in her brother's fear, breathes in her rage. Her talons flex in anticipation.

"Come, sisters," says Iphigenia, and they crow their assent, a cacophony of terrible, beautiful sound.

Iphigenia is the first to descend, her wings splayed out to block the sun.

A Poem by Mack W. Mani

Mythic Blooms (Fatherless/A Vision)

i.

Papa sailed to Troy
before I learned to sing,
naming me and calling it
a job well done.

My mother had to keep her figure
to stop the beating hearts
of a hundred bastard men,
their hungry eyes
ground up against her.

She lived always by the dawns
and early morning bluster
fingers weaving tailored eyes
to mark the tide and time,
crafting weathervane prophecies
of storms to come.

She would tell me what they told
all the fatherless boys:
*Your papa got lost
on his way home from Troy.*

ii.

You know
I thought I saw him once,
out among the drowning,
down below the wavy margins
where the future wells
and gravity pulls
like ironwood tendrils
reaching.

Choked on seawater,
flashes of my father
bathed in light
viridian and orchid pink,
monsters, naiads, sirens,
Scylla & Charybdis,
a man, a pig, a strapping fellow,
a nobody with a shock of golden hair,
lost alone
and caught
among the mythic blooms

Six Years After the Wedding

by Joe R. Christopher

Two Audio Versions: Arthur =Male Voice   Guinevere =Male Voice

Arthur: Our wedding is, on this sixth anniversary, still barren. You have not had so much as a miscarriage to suggest a possible later fulfilment. I need to have an heir to my throne. Two or three heirs—royal brothers—would be even better.

Guinevere: I know the wife is always blamed in this, her greatest duty; but surely it is as often the husband's fault as the wife's. The mysteries of conception are great secrets, largely unknown to us beyond classical cleverness and old wives' tales. And the wives, about the proper times between the periods, do not entirely agree.

Arthur: The latter does not matter, for I have seen to it that we have tried all the possibilities, including during your flow—as you well know.

Guinevere: You did not answer the former point.

Arthur: You must be desperate to say it is—or at least may be—the husband's fault. You've heard the wide-spread gossip: that I lay with my half-sister, Morgause, and engendered a boy—the same Mordred who came with my relatives to visit during the last Beltane. If necessary, I'll name the bastard my legal heir. So no, no, you cannot say this lack of children is my fault. I have proved myself.

Guinevere: Surely you cannot be certain that Morgause was faithful to you then, since she is promiscuous now.

Arthur: I have fair evidence during the period of engendering—we were youthful lovers, and greatly celebrating what we had discovered. My evidence is as good as most husbands have. I accept Mordred's appearance as resembling mine.

Guinevere: So you have decided against me.

Arthur: Not immediately, but I need an heir. Keep that in mind. After I finish the present war in Brittany, I will make a decision. You have the next few nights and perhaps a short while immediately afterwards.

Guinevere: And it must be a boy and it must look like you—I know the rules of the game.

Arthur: Game, madam? It is no game.

Two Poems
by Meg Moseman

Deathwater, Day

— at thought's edge, past a mountain peak in pine, there is a fountain, terraced, calciferous — silent in the sun, save for a susurrus of ripples — I met a wretch who said:

the water and the wind in their meeting are the voices of those who come
a trickling only in silence, almost silence. the water, thin like air, cannot rot or quench
it is only clear reflection, soft on the life of those who come
it is the life of them, it takes their life and circles
bearing universal life through those who come
they become vessels made of glass, clear, unrestricting
the fountain has a hundred tiers, it is the bones of those who come
water trickles wind words, breaks them around arches
nets of heat between bare sun and water's whispering edge
grow solid, fix and freeze. sparks catch atoms of self like glitter in granite
self heat-pinned until there is no mind or time but stony blocks of sense
what is more than life is gold reflection held in water, no longer water, a fiery gold band beaching on bone as water
turns to air. the pale ones who remain
still only made to kneel, will lurch, hear laughter, see a woman, rosy, well
an infant when dawn ought to break, a dying crone when night should fall
she laughs and picks up golden chains, wears them round her neck, dancing
the sun, its motion stolen by her life, grows hollow, stale, inanimate
light radiates off arches, echoes off the hard blue sky
she is only what the dying see, she is in their eyes and minds
when they dissolve there is silence, sun.

— because I left uncaught, black mold will mar white arches, water from some earthly stream will contaminate — crows will come someday, clouds bearing rain, arches will shatter, water sink into earth, trees grow, as lichen breaks the bone to clay —

Deathwater, Dusk

Lead us past the murky lakes, where all is laid to rest and sunk in earth.
In overhanging twilight, seeking has no use, and understanding dies.
There, terror has no meaning. All is still except for memory's inward spiral.
The dead of centuries lie underneath. Above, no birds, no blooms, no flies,

no breeze, no frogs, but only leaden water and the algae on the banks,
a mud no foot has touched. A reed perhaps grows here or there, upon that wide
expanse, a blasted tree, and nothing more. The air hangs over, cold and dead.
Lead us past the lakes or we lie down, no doubt forever, at their side.

All is still except for memory, I wrote
    and perhaps except for this: it's said —
        on still and moony nights —
        or luminous gray dawns —
        bright, empty afternoons
        when not a living thing will stir to watch —

a fountain will rise,
        clear and glimmering,
        and with it, piping, men —
        if such they may be called —
        of pale leaves and twigs and icy thoughts.

First slow, and dead, those thoughts,
        but sewn into quick music
        to twirl high and green and catch the living mind
        that listens from afar in leafy dreams.

--Meg Moseman

Poster by Jillian Drinnon

Working Title

by S. Dorman

Mark Twain had gone into outer darkness on a comet, leaving his friend Jack Lewis at his desk musing on their *great* experience together—an awful vision of the crucifixion in which the crucified Christ was nothing but an insect. At length Lewis sat forward with pen and paper, and began work once more on his new book, *Bareface*. He was rapidly scratching and flourishing away when a blur of white light shot past the corner of his eye—and back again.

A voice from behind said, "I like that Queen you're inventing. She's my kind of Queen, all bursting with ripe questions nobody can answer. Not even, apparently, God. Or at least he's not talking. Maybe by and by. It's easy, isn't it, having her pose all those difficult questions?"

There was another blur of white, a jet of quick cold as from absolute zero, and Lewis knew that his friend had gone back out into outer darkness... without him. He looked around at the full bookcases, the reading chair and lamp, papers scattered on the desk, seeing with relief that everything was as it should be, nothing had been disturbed. *When is he going to stop this*, wondered Lewis, gazing out latticed panes at a blossoming branch in the garden beyond the study at The Kilns. Then his musing deepened, and he thought, *When is he going to take me with him?*

Brrr.

"They will have this thing called 'string theory,' those mathematicians... popular in just a few decades too, Lewis. I'm not sure it will help your barbarian queen any, however. ...Maybe it's why I can come and go like this... while you have to stay here."

But Lewis looked for the source of the voice in what was now a roomful of smoke. He coughed a few times and cleared his throat. Those Havanas were good, perhaps, but not at secondhand.

"Particles of matter don't seem to occupy space with one another," said the smoke. "You can walk through the smoke, displacing bits, but you won't be able to walk through that wall over there... unless you climb out the window.

Well, it's all wonderful, and calculus is wonderful, mathematics... even as I must devise analogies to help me grasp it. Incomprehension doesn't keep me from participating. That's because I happen to be energy, with a touch of dark matter. Yes, don't look at me like that. I am energy. You, Lewis, are practically all matter."

Lewis, however, could not look, could not *see* a thing. He was enveloped in thick clouds of smoke, and burning ash and fulmination of particles/stars.

"Lewis," the disembodied voice was saying, "I've had to change my line of attack. For the moment I'm removing my sights off God, placing them more firmly on a corrupt and gullible humanity — and all the apparatus it's making for itself and its ambitions. This may be a temporary feature of the ongoing argument I have with Him. Since we've been having these conversations, and especially since that revelatory experience of the crucifixion we had here beneath the reading lamp...and for other considerations...I'm leaving that alone for now."

"Good," said Lewis, recovering from a coughing fit. "Perhaps you can do something about the atmosphere in here, as well?" But he was thinking about his barbarian queen and how tired he was of her carping continually on the subject of the gods—everything that was wrong with the gods, and how they wouldn't answer...over and over again. It was beginning to wear on him. Maybe he'd chuck the story if she didn't stop soon.

"God, as you say, or as we saw in a figure or vision or whatever it was, takes full responsibility for the monstrosity he created. Man. Human beings. There are the suffering, and there are those who cause the suffering, and often they are one and the same. Suffering? Why, there's a God... and he suffered like a bug pinned to a board for a scientist's scrutiny. But *still* there remains suffering of every stripe. ...Was that a pun?

"By the way, you have the knack of making me care for that queen and her sister, Psyche. Not like with that story of Stevenson's, _Prince Otto_, which also began with a mythical kingdom, not quite here nor there, but on the European fringes, old European—not an outlier of the aging classical Greece like you've got there. Stevenson's shows a lot of care in the telling, but I couldn't care myself for any of the characters.

"—And what did you think of _The Strange Case of Dr. Jekyll and Mr. Hyde_? I said that Hyde and Jekyll are the God of the Old and New Testaments, the split personality defined.... But!—I did say I was leaving that alone, so I'll make it *humanity* that is Jekyll/Hyde. Stevenson got it wrong, for the two persons inside a man are wholly unknown to each other and can never in this world communicate with each other in any way."

"Clemens," said Lewis with marked restraint, "*will* you get out of here and take that awful stuff with you. My eyes are watering and I can hardly breathe." His chair scraping the floor, he struggled past the desk to the window, fumbling and shoving it wide with a squeal. He hung out the window gasping, his hand on the latch, resting his wet gaze a moment on the blossomed branch. When he looked back his study was completely clear of smoke and smell. It was a clean wholesome fresh place again, full of books and birdsong from the garden.

His gaze fell to the desk and he noticed there a strange book, open to the middle, one of its pages silently turning. He went and stood peering down on it, expectantly, but instead of seeing black lines on the white page he heard the book itself uttering as though from a vast distance, faint and echoing. "I would still like to see the result of that sacrifice. The graves opened and everybody walked! Because, Lewis, you should see what the Hadleyburg 'meritocracy,' as they will call themselves, are doing around the time they develop this string theory with mathematics. It makes Theodore Roosevelt's handling of the Philippines and Chamberlain's of South Africa look like Fairday in Hannibal, Missouri."

27

A few more pages turned and the voice receded further, saying, "Your finest hour was also your last hour. Oh, England has a role to play in the so-called Cold War but it'll be a corrupting one. Extending the Blessings of Civilization and Christianity to our Brother Who Sits in Darkness has been a good trade and has paid well, on the whole; and there is money in it yet, if carefully worked— more territory, more sovereignty, and other kinds of emolument than there is in any other game that is played. But Christendom has been playing it badly of late years, and must certainly suffer by it, in my opinion."

The pages had been slowly turning themselves but now they turned with rapidity and finally a slam of the cover. Lewis stood a moment, staring down at the book, listening intently. No sound but garden birdsong. Perhaps the pest really was gone this time. It was an antique book, maybe 50 years old with brown dusty cover and gold lettering: *The Man That Corrupted Hadleyburg and Other Stories* by Mark Twain.

He knew better. He should not take time out from his busy day. There was a lecture to prepare, correspondence to answer, a hoped-for glass with Joy at the Bird and Baby, and then that commute. Now he glanced down at his own manuscript and then back at the Hadleyburg book. He picked it up, went over to the chair hard by the opposite window, and began to read.

Lewis raised his baggy eyes absently, thinking of the phrase about letting none escape unhurt. It put him in mind of Odysseus returning home to Penelope's suitors. He glanced down again and read on:

"The doors, the doors—close the doors; no Incorruptible shall leave this place!"

Well it's good, the author of *Bareface* said to himself. The myth comes out whole ... of a piece ...if the avenger *is* bitter. One rather wishes he were holy instead of bitter... but then considering the author, a real devil's advocate.... No, perhaps it wouldn't work any other way.

A movement outside caught his attention and he turned to see Samuel Clemens attired in his crisp white suit entering the garden gate. Lewis went to the other side of his desk to look out. The great American humorist was strolling around the garden, smoking his cigar. The white figure with its fluffy crown of white hair shone softly like a pearl in the fine soft air of the moist English spring morning. Life was gently stirring everywhere—in the swift short thin greens emerging from dark soil, the blossoming of various trees and shrubs, and in the hymn-singing of Wexford, The Kilns' gardener, hoeing in some corner. Of course he would not notice Samuel Clemens standing there: Wexford's imagination ran on the practical and dismal, for all the "Abide with Me" he exuded now. But everything responded to Spring, the practical and sublimely pointless alike.

"Can Odysseus have been such an admirable avenger? He stayed away from his wife for twenty years—was it?—and then expected her to be faithful."

Twain said this, standing beneath the white-blossomed branch, its black wet bark contrasting darkly in the faintly opalescent air. The smoke of his cigar wove itself up through delicate whitened branches, gently mingling with the mist. Wexford was singing, lugubriously, out of sight somewhere behind the yellow forsythia and other flowering shrubs.

Twain looked at him from beneath the blossoming tree. "No doubt God expects his bride to be faithful. But, like your queen, like Jekyll and Hyde, like Hadleyburg—we just can't seem to recognize ourselves. Oh yes, we are truly beside ourselves and don't even see ourselves standing there."

"Well, is it meant for a literary device, this non-recognition of the self, or do you believe we truly can't know the nature of self, the double self? Because it's all balderdash. We can get to know the self well if we're watchful. And I know *you* are, because I've read your 'Carnival of Crime...' and some other things revealing of this. No one could write as you do, in 'Letters from the Earth', about the secret supplications of the heart who is not aware of it."

There was a pause and then Lewis reached for the lattice, saying, "I've a lot to do... if you'll pardon me." Suddenly into the dripping stillness the voice of Wexford, rumbling and low, sang, " 'Prayer for weather mercifully tempered to the needs of the poor and the naked—Denied. This was a Prayer-Meeting prayer. It conflicts with item 1 of this report, which was a Secret Supplication of the heart—for weather to advance hard coal $.15 a ton—Granted.' "

Lewis stared in the direction of the bushes. He looked back at Twain. "Does he know he's doing that, singing that?—that quotation from the recording angel to the Buffalo, New York, coal dealer in your 'Letters from the Earth'?"

Clemens looked back at him with glimmering eyes. "Do you know it? I may be nothing but a dream. But in that case, who's having it?"

Editor's note: *Bareface* was the working title of C. S. Lewis' book that eventually became *Till We Have Faces*.

Twigman 2, by Meg Moseman

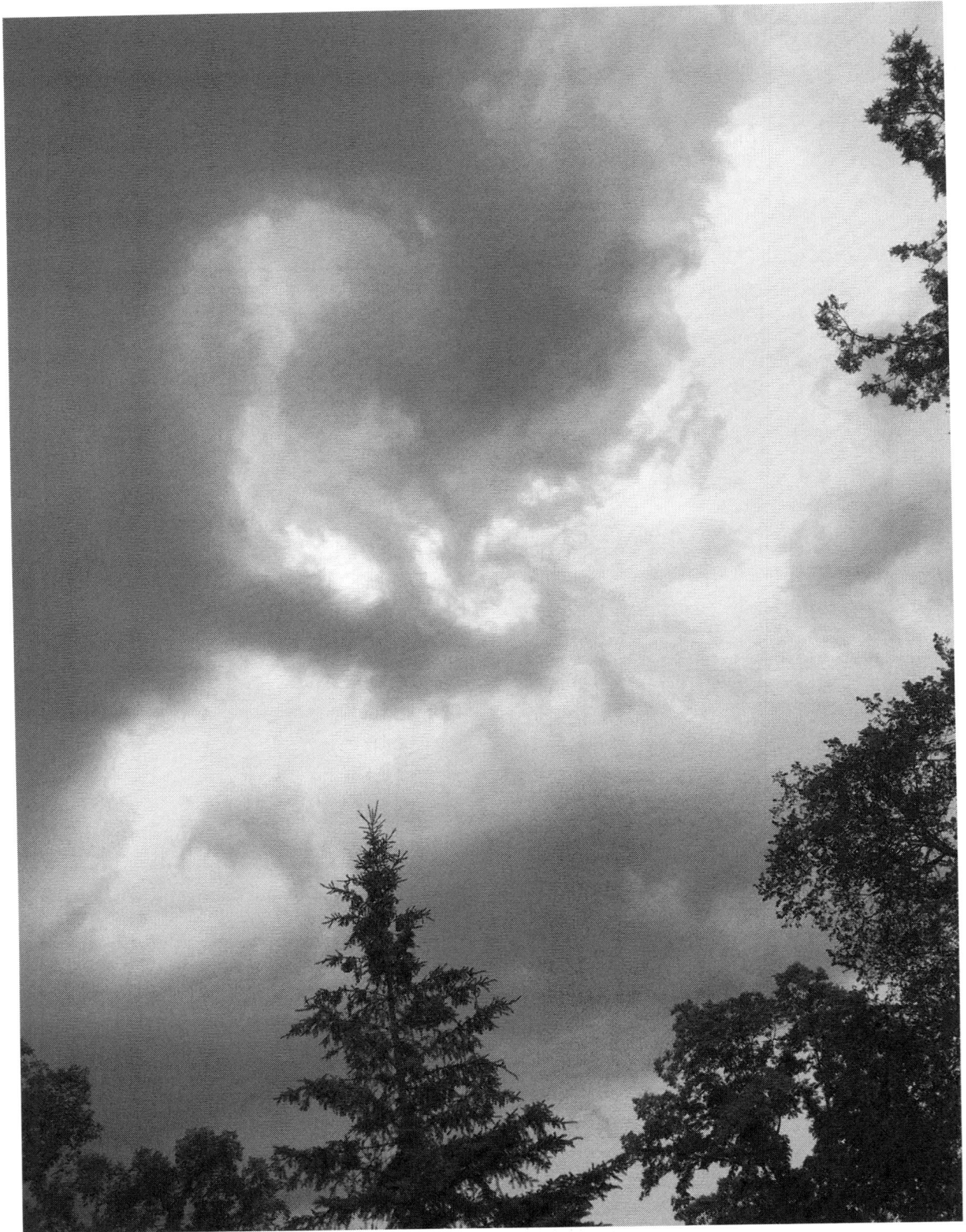

Menace, by Janet Brennan Croft

Two Poems by Holly Day

Loss

I look for it everywhere, the magic
I used to see around me. I carefully check
beneath cushions before I vacuum
approach dark, spiderwebbed corners with gentle hands lie awake to the sound of the house settling
the mice scampering in the attic, holding my breath hoping that it's there.

I watch my daughter playing in the yard
singing to earthworms and dancing with toads
and I know she sees all the magical things
I'm missing. I join in on her games
make fairy houses out of mud and broken seashells

share stories of how wonderful it would be
if we were frogs or fairies ourselves
and I can tell she believes
we could be those things if we really wanted to be that being just what we are is some sort of choice I can
tell she believes this

and I wish I could, too.

The Ship of Fools

If you see a bird in a tree, don't bother shooting at it. Sometimes, birds
shed their feathers of their own accord, willingly, before letting their head
fall to the ground and releasing all their organs. If you're patient enough, the sun will cook the meat right up
there, where the bird sits and waits, roast it to a fine golden perfection, until the
tips of the naked

wings sizzle and turn black. Only then will it make sense to climb up the thin, quaking branches
to release the bird, cut it down from the rubber bands binding it
to the tree, surrounded by sprigs of flowering sage and Spanish thyme. The men sitting around
the table below you are too busy chasing the bread loaves hanging
from the lower branches

to notice you have a roast pheasant under your arm. Their songs are all about the starving naked,
about boats moored in dry meadows, about why women aren't
allowed at their gatherings. You alone will truly feast tonight, and that is why this
poem is about you.

Troll

by Kevan Kenneth Bowkett

Once upon a time there lived a troll who guarded a tollbooth on a bridge.

He wasn't actually a troll but he was so stocky and ugly that everyone called him "Troll." Of course, because of this his place was called the Trollbooth.

Also, he couldn't see very well so he squinted a lot in order to see properly, and this made him even uglier, so people called him a "troll with a goblin face."

One day, a man in a hurry sold him a pair of shoes. They were bright yellow, but shabby, with green tongues. The tollbooth-keeper (we will call him Troll) put them on and thought himself the handsomest-turned-out fellow in the province. "I'll bet I could even walk into the presence of His Presence the Emperor in these shoes. They might—they might even be so handsome he'd want to buy them off me. Then I could buy my own tollbooth with my earnings." (He worked as an employee in the tollbooth and got a percentage of tolls, but he had ambitions, as you see).

So he went on thinking these thoughts of financial success, and walking back and forth across the bridge between the two heavy gates of the tollbooth as he usually did. It was a quiet time, and presently he noticed that a place in the heel of the left shoe was rubbing. He shook his foot and walked on. But soon he felt a sensation beneath his left heel, as if he were walking on a pebble. The sensation grew into a pain as he clumped back and forth across the bridge, but he ignored it, not wanting to find any fault with the shoes. But after a while the pain was too biting to ignore, so he sat down on his stone bench and pulled off his left shoe. It pulled off a little, but it wouldn't come much. He panicked and pulled hard, and the shoe came away, but he screeched as he felt what seemed a long thorn being yanked out of his heel. He looked in the shoe. Nothing like a thorn. He felt about. He could feel nothing but the bottom and sides and tongue of the shoe.

"Well this is a most peculiar strange shoe," he said in disgust. "What useless things, shoes." But he had spent good money on the shoes, so he put it on and rose, and started clumping back and forth again. The pain returned swiftly, and he hobbled to his bench, sat, and pulled at the shoe. He had to exert a great deal of strength to pull it away, and it felt like he was removing a red-hot meat-cooking skewer from his heel.

"That's enough of that shoe for me," he said, and threw the shoe against the bridge parapet.

"Ouch!" shouted a voice.

"Who's that?" said Troll, jumping up and hopping on one foot.

"It's me, the shoe," said the voice.

Troll hopped over to where the shoe lay on its side on the bridge, and bent down to peer inside it. "What are you doing in the shoe?" asked Troll, even though he could see nothing unusual.

"I'm not in the shoe," said the voice. "I *am* the shoe."

"Shoes don't talk," said Troll. "Shoo, you!" he added.

"But I'm here to shoe you," said the shoe.

"No thanks. You're too painful," said Troll.

"If you kept me on, the pain would diminish," said the shoe.

"No, I would diminish," said Troll, stooping and removing the remaining shoe.

"You would increase," coaxed the shoe, and the one Troll had just removed seemed to make faint echoing noises when the first shoe spoke. "You would look sharp, and smart, and earn more money, and be trusted with a loan, and buy your own toll gate—and then you could buy a dozen pairs of shoes, and take me off."

"I'll never be able to get you off by then," said Troll. "Unless I saw off my feet."

"But if you don't put me on, how will I get into the Emperor's presence? It's the only way for me to travel."

"You could walk," said Troll.

"I can only walk on someone's feet," said the Shoes.

"No one will let you, you hurt so much," said Troll. "Why were you so hard to get off? It felt like you wanted to eat me up."

"I only gripped on and tried to pull at your sole because I missed my master so much, and someone's foot is the only way to get to him, and your foot is better than the air's," said the Shoes. "The air doesn't take me anywhere."

"Haha, I like that!" said Troll. "When no one is wearing you you're on the air's foot! Haha!" And he guffawed again. Then, "Where is your master?" asked Troll, in a better humor.

"Only the Emperor knows," said the Shoes. "That's why I want to get to see the Emperor."

"Well," said Troll, his imagination growing full again, "if that's how it is, I can help you after all. I will take you round my neck. I will walk to the Emperor's palace. Then I will put you on to enter his presence, that is to say His Presence, since I must look my best, and you do look fine, that's why I bought you. But if you don't come off after I've put you on, I'll burn you off."

"It's a deal!" said the Shoes, and Troll shook one of the green tongues.
Troll filled a bag with food and bedding for the journey, tied the bright yellow shoes together by the laces, and put them round his neck. Then they faced toward the great and wonderful city of Cothirya, where the Emperor had his palace.

"Who'll watch the toll gates?" asked the Shoes.

Troll scratched his shoulder.

"Why do you scratch your shoulder and not your head?" asked the Shoes.

"A traveler told me people scratch their head to stimulate their intelligence," said Troll. "He helpfully added that my shoulder was more intelligent than my head. So I scratch it instead." He snapped his fingers. "I know!" he shouted, and rushed into his hut. In a moment, he reappeared carrying the skeleton of a human foot.

"This is from when a troll really did live under the bridge," said Troll. He waggled the metatarsal joints fondly, and then placed the bones on his stone bench that stood by the hut. "It's a toll gate, he said. "So it will be fine if it's a *toe gate* until we get back." And he guffawed again, and slapped the shoes on their backs.

They set off.

Over river and meadow and under mountain-wall they went, and through wood and dale, and beneath dawn and sunset. And after many adventures they came to Cothirya on its three hills above the inlet of the sea people call the East Gong.

They entered the city.

Troll was dazzled by the number of people, the noise, the smells, the huddled wooden houses and tenements, the soaring towers and palaces, the size of the place. In one square he saw more people than he had ever seen in his whole life before.

But the Shoes guided him through it, and they came presently to a quiet courtyard full of refuse, which was more congenial to Troll's nerves. There, sitting on an old packing crate that smelt of blue mongoose, Troll put the Shoes on.

Then they went to the Palace.

The guards, in bright armour and billowing golden cloaks, and carrying flashing spears and swords, stopped him and demanded his business.

"I've come to the capital to get the worser of the Emperor," said Troll, and the Shoes made him dance a jig.

The guards laughed and their captain said, "Don't you mean get the *better* of the His Presence the Emperor?"

"That too," said Troll.

"Well, the shoes you are wearing are fine enough to get you admitted," said the captain. "But the rest of you is a touch raggedy."

"He is a raggedy jester, ma'am," said a guard to the captain, and some of the others chimed in, concurring.

The captain smiled and said, "I think so, too. You may enter."

It was, in any event, the one day of the decade when anyone might be admitted to the Emperor's Presence. (It had used to be the one day in a month, but things had changed.)

Troll had to speak to several officials and be danced in a jig or a hornpipe by the Shoes several times before he was finally admitted to the Presence of the Emperor of Cothirya.

The last official he was forced to placate to be admitted to the Presence was the Master of Ceremonies who, having seen more than his fill of dancing, demanded a pleasant tale as Troll's price of admission. So Troll told the story of "The Dragon in High Heels." The Master of Ceremonies was pleased at Troll's story, and admitted him at once to the imperial throne room.

It all seemed a great bright golden glow to Troll, but the Shoes made him walk over to stand before a man on a high throne made of malachite. The Shoes nipped Troll's little toes, so he came to his senses enough to make as stately a bow as he could, so low that some of the ragged strips of his clothing brushed the floor.

The man on the throne – His Presence the Emperor – looked down at this person before him and said, "Those are some very fine shoes that you are wearing, master."

"I am not wearing the shoes," said Troll. "The shoes are wearing me."

The Emperor laughed.

"They would make a fine gift to My Presence," he said presently. "And should you give them to me, well: one good turn oft brings on another."

"Like this!" cried Troll, and the shoes took him several elegant but comic turns across the floor, which was made of carefully ground and polished coral. The Emperor laughed again, and clapped.

"Those shoes I must have," he said.

Troll bent and unlaced the Shoes, and placed them together before His Presence the Emperor's throne, with the heels toward His Presence, then backed away, bowing.

Two servants came and each one took a shoe and laced it quickly onto one of the Emperor's feet without touching him.

Then the Emperor stood; and the Shoes took him in a swift caper across the floor. The Emperor laughed.

"This is wonderful!" cried the Emperor. "In these shoes I am light on my feet as a rhea's feather!"

But the Shoes made him dance faster, and then faster yet, and then still faster, until the Emperor was a coloured whirlwind, and he called out, "Stop, Shoes!"

The Shoes stopped. The Emperor looked tired and was wet with perspiration. Servants ran to him with towels and iced sherbet, but the Shoes whisked him away from them, then stopped him on the other side of the throne room.
"Release my master, and I shall release you!" cried the Shoes.

"I have not seized your master," said the Emperor.

"That troll-like but estimable fellow is not my master," said the Shoes. "My master is the merchant Athro the Master Cobbler. You have his soul sealed up in a glass jar somewhere."

"I don't negotiate with shoes," said the Emperor, seeing his warriors approach. "Or even with Shoes."

The Shoes immediately took His Presence on a long very quick-paced springle-ring, deftly avoiding the clutching fingers of the astonished guards, and dancing him up back onto his throne, where no one was permitted to approach him. The Shoes dumped him into his seat and then flung themselves, and his legs, up over the right-hand arm of the throne, so that the Emperor was immobilized.

Meanwhile the warriors had encircled Troll, but he was too enthralled by the spectacle to notice. He stood, arms crossed, enjoying the sight, and resolving to soon come again to Cothirya where such interesting things were on view.

"Now!" cried the Shoes. "Release my master!"

"There is no need for coercion," said the Emperor, huffing. "He's a trader. Let us trade, therefore. I keep you and you obey me, and I release him."

"That's better," said the Shoes. "And another condition: give my troll-like friend a hundred silver sovereigns so that he can buy his own troll gate—toll gate. And refrain from proceeding against him for his part in this."

"Very well," said the Emperor. He snapped his fingers, and the warriors stepped back from Troll, who was chuckling and shaking his head.

"Now, my master," said the Shoes.

"I will have to walk to where he is," said His Presence.

"Walk on," said the Shoes.

The Emperor rose, and crossed the throne room, and went out a door, preceded by the two servants and followed by Troll and six guards. They went along various passages and up some helical stairs, and came to a large chamber with a balcony overlooking a garden.

In the middle of the chamber there was a big apparatus covered with a white cloth with blue birds embroidered on it. The Emperor pulled a cord and the cloth fell away, revealing a gigantic golden trident as long as two men, that lay upon three silver brackets on wood posts about one leg high. Troll chuckled and shook his head, while the Emperor went into a closet and came back with a jar of dark green glass. This he placed on a table before the trident. He removed the wooden stopper and immediately there leaped a beam of green light from the mouth of the jar to the tines of the trident. The beam bent round one of the tires, then continued on through the casement and curved down into the garden.

"Release his soul from the jar," said the Shoes.

"He's released now that the stopper is off," replied the Emperor. "But he seems to be sleeping."

He lightly tapped the glass with a fingernail. After a second, a bright green mote of light appeared. It paused in the air above the jar, and then shot away along the beam of light, which vanished behind it as it went. It slipped among the tines of the trident, then zipped to the casement and down into the garden.

"It will take a few minutes for him to awake and come to us," said the Emperor.

"It's a fine show," said Troll.

"I agree," said the Emperor. "That's why I do it. When anyone displeases me sufficiently, I take the trident, jab their soul with it, and draw it out and put it in a jar, as you see. Their body then sleeps in that garden until I deem their punishment complete. Then I release them."

"A fine show," said Troll.

"We'll be having more releasing and less punishing with me on your feet," said the Shoes.

In a few minutes, a tired but pleased-looking man came up the stairs from the garden to the balcony, and nodded to the Shoes. Various strips of leather and hanks of twine hung from his belt, showing that he was a cobbler.

"You bargained?" he said.

"I did," replied the Shoes.

"Well. Wear well, of course. And I'll make something to buy you back with, if I can," said the cobbler.

"Oh, master!" cried the Shoes, and made a squeaking sound like weeping.

"What a place!" cried Troll, and roared with laughter.

And that was how Troll visited the Emperor, and the Shoes released their master. The cobbler went back to his work in the city. Troll was given a sack of a hundred silver sovereigns and, after spending one night sleeping on the floor of the cobbler's shop, returned home, where he found that all the travelers, confronted by the skeleton foot of a real troll's victim, had paid in full. By the next season Troll owned and was running his own toll gate, this one on a bridge over a narrow lake. He would fish from the bridge parapet, murmuring "What a show!" and planning for the day when he would again visit Cothirya, where such interesting things happen.

Twigman 3, by Meg Moseman

The Dreaded Tome of Urawn

by Lee Clark Zumpe

"Curse you, mortal," shouted the great gray dragon vexedly as the mortal on her back fidgeted nervously in his saddle. "By the gods, be still!"

Far from her lavish den in the Northern Mountains, the dragon soared through the sky above a leafy canopy. Zuignaar and her human attendant had traveled no small distance to reach the long-abandoned city of Arrahkeesh in the wilds of the Nairuvian jungle. Therein, she hoped to find and secure a dangerous manuscript, the very existence of which caused dire concern among the Council of Elder Dragons.

High in the evening sky, the dragon's sharp eyes could only now discern the bubbling domes and towering minarets of the ancient stronghold silhouetted against the fading traces of the sunset. Friel clutched anxiously at her hide, still trembling from the storm-darkened skies through which they had pressed to make the city before nightfall.

"Can you see it yet?" he asked excitedly.

"Yes, I can see it. We'll be there in a matter of moments," the dragon said, reassuring him with a softer tone of voice than she had used a moment earlier when she had reprimanded him. Though she hated to admit it, she liked little Friel and found herself exceedingly reluctant to censure him in any way. She had never developed such a fondness for one of her slaves. "I'll have you safely down on your precious ground shortly."

The black walls of Arrahkeesh rose up arrogantly out of the tangle of an untamed jungle. Long had those walls gone unattended by guardians, and long had the watchtowers been vacant. Only the jungle itself now threatened the city whose kings and citizenry had disappeared ages ago. Zuignaar knew that even thieves shunned this sinister place, and that the prize that she sought would not be easily won.

As the dragon lit upon the rain-sodden cobblestone surface of the city's central square, Friel silently offered up a prayer of thanks to the patron god of adventures, Ulahn.

Dark towers and long-deserted temples stood silent. Streets, overrun with probing vines from the encroaching jungle, trailed off into a tangle of terraced archaic masonry haunted by shadows and legends. Overseeing the deserted streets, the citadel of the ill-famed wizard Urawn crouched upon the crest of a ridge that enfolded the city. Zuignaar wondered if the screams of Urawn's sacrifices still echoed through the halls of that fortress, if the spatters of blood still stained the marble floors of his conjure-cells.

From the ledge of a nearby edifice, a row of grim-faced gargoyles glared down at the gray dragon and her man-servant.

"I've not ever seen a city such as this," Friel whispered, fearful that his voice might rouse spirits of the dead. He marveled at the unusual architecture, the intricate designs adorning each building, the somber statues quietly guarding the entrance to each building. Open-mouthed he wondered at the complexities of patterns, at the vastness of it all. "Certainly this place was not built by human hands," he finally declared, looking toward his master for enlightenment.

"Aye, it was," Zuignaar answered calmly as she scanned the crumbling walls. "Built in the Age of the Yellow Moon, when the Faceless King ruled from the throne high atop the cliffs of Mount Ty'Ryluan. The walls of this city were raised very long ago, before the Wars of the Goblin Clans, and before the Scarlet Plague descended upon your race."

"And the dragons allowed it?" Friel asked, his eyebrows rising in disbelief. The slave could not accept that his scrawny, feeble-minded kin could erect such a colossal fortification, nor could he believe that the dragons would permit such a city's construction.

"Well, er," the gray dragon began, trying to find a satisfactory response that would urge no further inquiries, "The city, you see, was built before the dragons had formed the confederation. In those days, the Emperor permitted the establishment of some settlements to see whether or not freed humans could live independently. It was nothing more than an experiment, one which clearly failed." Zuignaar smiled a little, inadvertently flashing her dagger-length fangs. "Once the confederation had been founded, the Council of Elder Dragons quickly outlawed mortal colonies— which, I think, was for the best."

"Oh," Friel said, accepting the explanation at face-value. He struck out into the shadows hesitantly, poking his head down a gloomy alley. "What happened to everyone that lived here, then?"

"Dead, I'm sure," Zuignaar answered quickly. She kept an eye on her slave as he investigated the ruins, but in the meantime she withdrew a piece of parchment from a satchel on her back. Upon the scroll was a detailed map of the city, along with a few verses written in the language of the Old Wyrms. Only learned dragons could translate such ancient runes. "We know little about the fate of this city other than what was recorded in an old book—" The dragon caught herself. She realized she had almost told her servant about the mortal-penned Tome of Rathnik. The Council would have had her spiked tail for such a blunder. Humans simply did not read and write.

"A book?" the slave mumbled.

"Yes," she said, glancing at the slave as he wrestled with a heavy door. She found a bitter taste upon her tongue with each new lie, but knew she could not reveal the truth to Friel no matter how much she trusted him. "More like a journal, really—kept by a reclusive dragon. It reports that the city was sacked by some nameless legion from the deep jungle before the dragons could come and lead the humans back to safety in the heart of the empire."

"Such a tragedy," Friel said, grimacing. He rammed his shoulder against the stubborn door one last time before giving up. "It goes to show, though," he said as he wandered back to Zuignaar's side,

"That humans must not strike out on their own. They are best kept by their masters, protected from the bad things of the world."

"Precisely," the gray dragon said, nodding her head. "Now, I believe that the shrine we seek should lie down this avenue—"

"Perhaps someday," Friel said absently, interrupting the dragon, "Humans will be ready to leave the roost, though. Dragons and humans could live together, not as master and servant, but as equals."

"I don't know about—"

"—and humans could build new cities, cities as big as this one—only more splendid, and far less gloomy."

"Friel," the gray dragon said firmly, "We have much to do. We haven't the time to dream silly dreams." The Council of Elders had entrusted this important task to Zuignaar knowing that she would not disappoint them. She would not allow her feelings for her slave to jeopardize the success of her quest. "I know I can depend on you."

"Yes, Zuignaar," the human said solemnly, bowing to his master. "I am sorry."

"Let us find the Shrine of the Black Monolith and secure the tome. Then we can leave this accursed place and never set eyes upon it again."

The two set out down the avenue cautiously, knowing that the spawn of the savage jungle could stalk these streets. Moonglow provided some light, but failed to disperse the gloom from many corridors. Zuignaar shot delicate ribbons of fire into some of the more ominous shadows, scattering the darkness long enough to assure her slave that nothing monstrous or menacing lurked there.

Friel hiked bravely down the increasingly narrow city streets while Zuignaar hopped from perch to perch atop the fast-decaying buildings on either side. She took great care when she set down on the old buildings, knowing that her weight might be enough to collapse any one of them and to send a shower of debris raining down into the street and upon her servant.

Zuignaar shuddered to think what she would do if any harm were to come to her little Friel.

"I think I've found it," the slave cried out. "The pillars are of the darkest stone I've ever seen—as though they were cut from dusk itself."

"That is it! Those are the Columns of Haydin the Wicked, first priest of the Black Monolith." The gray dragon found a sturdy landing place and stretched her long neck down into the street where Friel stood. "See the nine steps of black marble," she asked, her voice quivering with thrill of discovery, "and the thirteen nesting gargoyles perched atop the crest of the temple?"

"They are hideous, those things," the slave said, eyeing the uncanny sculptures teetering on the ledge high above him. Glaring downward with vengeful eyes were thirteen mammoth winged demons cut from the same black stone that had begot the columns, the stairway and the monolith itself. "What made them forge such horrible things?"

"The evil of this place, of the Black Monolith itself, twisted their minds and made them create such abominations in the name of their gods." The dragon regarded the gargoyles uneasily, their stony wrath disquieting her. "All around this city you will find such loathsome things—but these thirteen are the most malignant of them all, for Urawn himself carved them from the black stone."

"I do not understand," the slave said, shrugging his shoulders and scowling.

"Do not let it trouble you," Zuignaar told her favorite slave, nudging him gently toward the steps with her snout. "Now take your firebrand and enter this place—walk to the center of the temple and you shall find an altar. Upon that altar is the Tome of Urawn." She snorted and puffed smoke from her gaping nostrils. "Bring the book to me, and then we can leave."

"It is so dark inside—can we not wait for the dawn?"

"No, little one," she said, "I cannot bear to stay here a moment longer than I must. If you are afraid, call out and I will answer."

Friel hesitantly entered the temple, the light of his torch shimmering on the walls of polished black stone. Dust layered the floor, and a handful of bats clinging to the ceiling stirred and shrieked at the unexpected intrusion. The dragon watched apprehensively as he passed through the archway and faded from view. The rampant darkness inside quickly swallowed all trace of his torch.

"Friel!" Zuignaar called out only a moment later, already worried about her servant, "Friel, can you hear me?"

"I can," the slave answered promptly, "I am moving down a corridor toward the central chamber—I can see statues and fountains, and—"

"Yes," the dragon asked, frightened by the sudden silence. "What do you see?"

"The altar—and the dreaded Tome of Urawn!"

"That is wonderful," the dragon said. She sighed heavily and smiled. "Now bring it to me."

Friel did not respond for several instants, and the warmth of the dragon's victory began to grow cold.

"Friel?" Zuignaar quit her perch and flapped her wings nervously, hovering above the temple while she bowed her head closer to the entrance to try to find her slave. "Friel, are you still there?"

"Yes, I am fine," Friel called out from the darkness. "I am going over a few of the passages in this text."

"What are you talking about?"

"I am reading," the slave said, and Zuignaar staggered in the air. One of her wings accidentally grazed a nearby building and bricks tumbled into the street. "Do not be angry with me—not all humans are illiterate, you know."

"But the elders do not permit humans to—"

"No, the Council of Elder Dragons does not allow humans to do much of anything. They certainly don't approve of sharing the truth about our history with us." Zuignaar kicked aside the remnants of the building across the street from the temple so that she could draw even closer to the archway. She thrust her head through the massive doorway and stretched her neck down the corridor. "It is most fortunate that we humans have managed to pass on our history verbally from generation to generation, so that it is not forgotten how the dragons subjugated us after our numbers were depleted from the plague."

"You mustn't say things like that," the dragon pleaded as she strained to push a little deeper into the temple. "If you just bring me that book, I will explain everything."

"I do not think I am in need of your explanations anymore, old Zuignaar. I think I understand everything, now. Arrahkeesh was a secret city founded by escaped slaves—and Urawn was a sorcerer who learned that dragons had natural enemies of old, and he knew that if he could summon them, then he could liberate his people from their servitude. The Tome of Urawn provides the invocation to rouse our allies from their slumber."

"Friel, please," the gray dragon said. "I cannot bear to hear such blasphemies—don't force me to punish you, please!"

"You thought you could keep this from us," the human said bitterly. "You really believed that we would not grow tired of slavery. The time has come, master."

"Your kind could not have survived without us—"

"'Kah-rah, Alh-fahl, Kohnah, Ir.'"

"We gave you shelter, protected you from the goblins—"

"'Mah-rah, Kah-Han, Naguu, Ir.'"

"Friel," the gray dragon pleaded, "Don't read another word—"

"'Toh-mah, Sha-Toh, Nando, An.'"

Zuignaar shuddered. A ripple of activity raced across the city as things long-dormant awakened while the last syllable of Friel's summoning echoed through the halls of the temple. The dragon whimpered as she heard the sudden savage howls shatter the silence of the night. Ugly black wings fanned out beneath the twilight, dark eyes filled with fiery rage and stony faces twisted with anger.

As their spawn gathered in the skies above Arrahkeesh, the thirteen reigning gargoyles stared at the plump dragon before them and smiled.

At long last, the feast would commence.

Equuleus of Troy

by DC Mallery

In the waning days of The Trojan war, as Agamemnon's Army was losing hope, the Towering Horses of the wilds of North Africa were but myth and fable to both Greeks and Trojans. Only bards and balladeers and those driven mad with diseases of the mind swore the mighty steeds were *real*, that they had been harnessed in ancient times to build the colossal monuments of the Nile Valley and the many other Great Edifices of Ages past.

And that such massive steeds still lived. Few believed them.

But Odysseus had travelled far and seen many wondrous sights and was not so quick to dismiss those Mighty Horses as mere myth and folly. So, with the War nearing its tenth year, with even Achilles now dead, and the Siege of Troy seemingly endless, seemingly hopeless, Odysseus sent the trusted Epeius and his scouts south across the Mediterranean to the seaside village of Cyrene and the Deep Wilds that lay beyond, to find one of the those Stalwart Horses.

For Odysseus had a plan.

A Gift.

Not a gift to the foul Men of Troy, of course, for they had kidnapped fair Helen. No, an offering to the Goddess Athena, an offering to her so she might favor Agamemnon's Army in their battles and in their journeys home. The Trojans would arrogantly take the gift as their own. They flattered themselves as great horsemen, the horse the very emblem of Troy. King Priam's father—the deceitful Laomedon—once claimed to have magic horses, sent by the Gods themselves. The Trojans would learn that the Towering Steeds of The South were not magic, but flesh and blood, with strong hearts and even stronger wills. The Trojans would learn that The Greeks also had strong hearts and strong wills. And guile to spare. The Trojans would then feel the wrath of Agamemnon's Army and the even greater wrath of Athena herself.

And so a gift would be left pacing outside the gates of Troy. A gift hiding a deadly secret.

§

Even with favorable winds, it took weeks to transport the colossus by sturdy barge from North Africa to the Aegean coastline near Troy. The journey had been fraught with danger, but Poseidon had favored them. When Epeius arrived from Cyrene with the mighty beast, the men of Agamemnon's army gaped in awe, and their horses did too, both awed and humbled, for the massive steed stood ten-fold the height of a stout man, and his hooves shook the Earth as he came ashore, his eyes glistened like heavy wet stones, the hide thick, the muscles strong.

Soon, though, the men laughed at the beast, for he was no beast.
Equuleus was gentle, of a mild and temperate disposition, content to graze and meander along the brushy shores of the Aegean. Odysseus chastened the men, for this beast was not meant to use strength to tear down the walls of Troy, for not even a steed this powerful could cleave those ramparts. The horse would use bravery and guile to defeat those walls.

The men listened in wonder to Odysseus's plan. For along with the mighty steed, Epeius had brought a mysterious hippomancer from Cyrene, one of the magi, an enchanter. The man would call upon the benevolence of the Gods, of Athena herself, and a dozen strong Greek soldiers would be drawn beneath the skin of the Mighty Horse—absorbed through his hide, as a parched desert might soak up a spill of water—to then burrow between the massive ribs, to breathe through hollowed reeds that poked from the tough skin of the beast, to lie in wait there.

Agamemnon would order the tents of his weary army to be burnt. They would embark upon their fleet of ships, appearing to give up The Siege and leave for Greece, defeated, humbled. As the forces pretended to withdraw, one of Agamemnon's soldiers, he who was called Sinon, would lead Equuleus to the Gates of Troy. He would tell the Trojan guards that the beast was an offering for Athena, not them, that it was made magically large so it would not fit through the gates into the city. That they should not take it for themselves.

But, of course, they would. For treachery was in their very blood. They would take Equuleus inside the city.

§

The mighty steed knew nothing of the strange language of these Greeks, but the enchanter, the kind man who fed and groomed him, explained the brave role Equuleus was meant to play. He told him of the fair Helen, kidnapped and held captive for ten years. The steed wept at the story, for he had been so long from his own home, captured ages ago by Traders, taken far from his gentle pastures, enslaved. The man assured Equuleus that once the gates of Troy were open and the Trojans defeated, he himself would arrive to bind the steed's wounds with stout twine and strong magic. It would be as though the soldiers had never burrowed under his hide. He would rise, stronger than ever, the favorite now of Athena. He would be returned to his homeland to live out his long days in well-fed splendor under gentle skies.

§

And so it was done.

Under a moonless sky, as the army burned their tents and readied to sail, Equuleus hunkered low along the shore so armed men, their swords sheathed in scabbards, could be drawn under the thick hide. The enchanter brought down powerful magic, no doubt from Olympus itself, and the men were pulled under the skin to settle between the ribs, and it did not hurt the beast. Sinon lead Equuleus to the Gates of Troy. As planned, he told the guards the Mighty Steed was an offering for Athena, that it would be too large to fit through the gates into Troy.

"Take it into the city!" the Trojan guards exclaimed, for the gates were tall enough to bring even this massive beast inside, head bowed, strong legs bending low, the men hidden.

Equuleus was taken into a broad square inside the city walls. In the morning, Priam himself would want to see this great stallion!

Late that night, as the Trojan guards slept, Agamemnon's men withdrew their swords and cut their way from the chest of the beast. The pain was fierce, but the brave steed stifled his agonies for he knew not to awaken the city. As blood spilled from his open wounds, a dozen Greek soldiers dropped to the ground and slew all nearby, quick and merciless.

They opened the great gates of Troy. Agamemnon's army swarmed in.

The Trojan Men were brave too, the fighting brutal, and many were slain on both sides. Equuleus fought hard, crushing many of the enemy, taking countless arrows. His strength flagged as more and more of his blood was spilled. His mighty heart weakened.

By dawn, the Trojans were defeated and Priam was dead. The Great Steed waited for the enchanter to arrive to bind his wounds, to heal him, and waited. And waited.

It was not the first time a proud and innocent beast was betrayed by the wiles of Men. The enchanter never intended to return. Already sailing south, his job was done. Agamemnon's men abandoned Equuleus, too. They drank with gluttony and pillaged with righteous furor and took the many spoils of their victory. Even Odysseus had no time for the brave fallen steed.

Equuleus slumped to the ground, his massive lungs choked with blood, long limbs growing cold, mighty heart finally failing. Knowing he would not survive, he hoped to at least catch a glimpse of the fair Helen, the woman he had given his life for. He saw her not.

When at last Equuleus closed his eyes, those sad eyes did not again open. Not here.

§

Athena watched and Athena wept. As did the other Gods of Olympus.

For they too knew the folly and the betrayal of Men. They punished Odysseus for abandoning the Brave Steed to die, forcing him and his men to spend another ten long years on their journey home. The Gods vowed to never allow the mighty and massive stallions of The Deep South to ever again be tricked and betrayed as Equuleus had been in the Land of Troy.

With powerful magic, they shrunk all of those Towering Steeds, every last one, wherever they stood in the whole of The World, down to the size of mere horses.

For his heroism and his bravery, they chose to immortalize the Great Steed in the stars of the sky. But they bickered among themselves as to where and how large for there was little room in the night sky for another hero, and so it became one of the smallest of all constellations.

Equuleus.

In time, his deeds and his heroism were forgotten.

The brave sacrifice of the mighty steed fell into myth. As stories were handed down from one to another, the tale of that great living steed changed, bit by bit, word by word, line by line. In time, the brave Trojan Horse was not so massive and it was rolled into the city on a wooden cart, the men hidden inside the cart, not within the steed itself. Later, the story changed yet again, the Trojan Horse now made of wood, the men hidden inside that contrivance.

So the great Towering Equuleus—Brave and Mighty and Alive—was replaced in the tales of Homer and Virgil by nothing more than a contraption of wooden planks and rusted nails.

Even his name, Equuleus, was lost from the lore and hymns of The Trojan War. In time, the connection between his namesake constellation and his heroic deeds was forgotten, too.

The Gods of Olympus might have wept at this, as well, but they too were reduced to myth, mere tales told to children: fables, legends.

Alas, Mighty Equuleus was not the last brave and heroic horse to be led into battle by Men, not the last to suffer, not the last left to die on a battlefield, abandoned.

Ever since, Equuleus has looked down upon all war horses and battle steeds.

He is proud to know that, in their hearts, the power of his mighty heart still pounds.

Twigman 1, by Meg Moseman

Epic

A back-to-the-future Shamanic telling for public recitation
by David Sparenberg

Or visit the following URL:
https://www.youtube.com/watch?v=0UZTPmNwUr4&feature=youtu.be

Sing in me, Muse, the epic tale of that Earth daughter who shook the foundations of the Dark Towers and challenged in combat the dread lords of tyranny and their master the Patriarch of Death. Before the Book, back in The Dreaming—over eons of Shaman Lore—it is attested that light is restoration for those who are eaten by their own shadows and fire is the bane of phantoms. From somewhere here, Muse, begin.

The Woman-Warrior Princess, Ona TrueHeart, shook her beautiful head with the flowing locks. She shook her beautiful head topped by the shining helmet with the flowing plume of rainbow colors.

Ona lifted her invincible weapons of light and fire in an honoring gesture to All Fathering Sun. She chanted her kindred chant to Elder Sister Moon. She made a prayer offering to All Mothering Earth. Then Ona unleashed from her throat a furious battle cry—the battle cry that confounds wrongdoers who oppose her and shakes the foundations of injustice.

Ona TrueHeart mounted her winged horse with the flowing mane and tail. Feathers of the wing on the mount's left side were a pure radiance of golden-white light. Feathers of the wing on the mount's right side were a shimmering iridescence of rainbow colors.

Ona TrueHeart was one, yet she was many. She emerged from the Realm of the Mothers; she came out from the Council of All Beings. Behind her gathered the Guardians and Ancient Spirits who do not age. In the onslaught of batter, the Cosmic Green Dragon mirrored in her Woman-Warrior's heart breathes fire through her mouth and nostrils. In the onslaught of battle, lightning shoots from her spellcasting eyes.

Ona rode forth, in the direction of the Dark Towers of Power, seeking battle against the forces of evil. Myriad were the bright-eyed maidens, myriad the long-haired youth of the shires who pledged loyalty to the Woman-Warrior and followed her path on the Beauty Way.

When the battle cry of Ona TrueHeart rang out from her throat in thundering truth-force, it shook the foundations of the Dark Towers of Power. Gripped by prophetic fear, soothsayers and practitioners of black magic hastened to assemble in the grand hall of the Dark Lords.

Among the assembly of ministers, councilors, warlords, vassals, robber barons, assassins and astrologers, the richest and most powerful was first to speak. Sunken eyed and discolored with seething contempt, the dread lord proclaimed loudly, "Ona TrueHeart comes against us. She comes to do battle. She has emerged from the Realm of the Mothers; she comes out from the Council of All Beings. Ona is one yet she is many. Gathered to her are the Guardians and Ancient Spirits who do not age. Ona rides the winged horse. The Woman-Warrior bears the invincible weapons of light and fire."

The speaker paused as a stirring and grumbling rippled throughout the vast hall. The chief lord of corruption resumed: "She plans to put an end to the cruelty that is our power to govern. She plans to stop the wickedness by which we prosper. This Ona TrueHeart cannot be defeated. She comes in the prophecy made long ago by Land Dreamers and Water Dreamers and the Keepers of the Animals that have perished at our hands."

It was then that the eldest and most timorous of the Dark Lords cried frantically. "Let us flee. Quick! We must run! We must hide before we are taken captive and wealth and power are stripped from us."

"Yes," many agreed as panic took hold of the assembly. "To where shall we run? Where will we hide?" one among the stricken asked. Another of the Order of Dread and Terror added, "To what place where the light will not expose us? Even shadows that have served our every secret, now quake and are scattered and shrink before the woman's quickening approach, before the judgment of her battle cry!"

Hearing these words, voiced in the contagion of fear, the Patriarch of Death arose from his throne of skulls and bones and shouted menacingly a wrathful reproach. "Cowards! Cowards all! For generations our kind has held the world by the throat. How skilled we have been at war! How skilled in covert operations! In cunning, our order is unrivaled; unrivaled in the art of betrayals."

The Patriarch of Death cast a baleful eye at his followers, then resumed his proclamation. "Now are we to flee before a woman? This Ona TrueHeart is little more than a girl. She rides this way in search of victory. A contemptable gesture."

As the Ruler of Rulers spoke, the Dark Towers shook in their foundations a second time. Once again Ona had unleashed her furious battle cry that confounds wrongdoers who oppose her and shakes the foundations of injustice.

Upon this tremor, Master of the Dark Lords clutched his massive battle ax and swung it in rage over his head, next stabbing and hacking at the empty air before him. "Call out the armies!" the Patriarch commanded. "Assemble the battalions in battle formation!" He laughed cruelly and his laughter sounded like a storm rumbling through the great chamber. "Ona TrueHeart approached, dreaming of victory. She will receive defeat and death at our hands. Away! Make ready! This day we will drink the heart blood of Ona—a woman—lamb of the dreamers."

Ona arrived at the Dark Towers of Power; battle was joined—the battle between light and darkness, between good and evil, between life and death, between treachery and truth. In the onslaught the Cosmic Green Dragon mirrored in her Woman-Warrior's heart breathes fire from her mouth and nostrils. In the onslaught, lightning shoots from her spellcasting eyes.

Many are those in the ranks of corruption who yield before the Woman-Warrior's radiant light. Many are those who surrender to the beatitude of the Woman-Warrior's love. Victory is won through love's purity and courage   Only by love are the Dark Lords vanquished; the Dark Towers brought down to the shared abundance of Earth and the Patriarch of the Order of Dread and Terror forever exiled from the decency of the world.

A Poem
by David Sparenberg

Ritual

Here is the place of the big tree
Here is the place of coming together
Known as the Ring of Gathering

Here people stand in circle
Here we join hands
Faces bright with morning sun
Faces beam from smiling moon

Here people dance a circle dance
Here people sing to Earth and Sky

Here is the place of memory
Here we are happy
In the place of the towering tree.

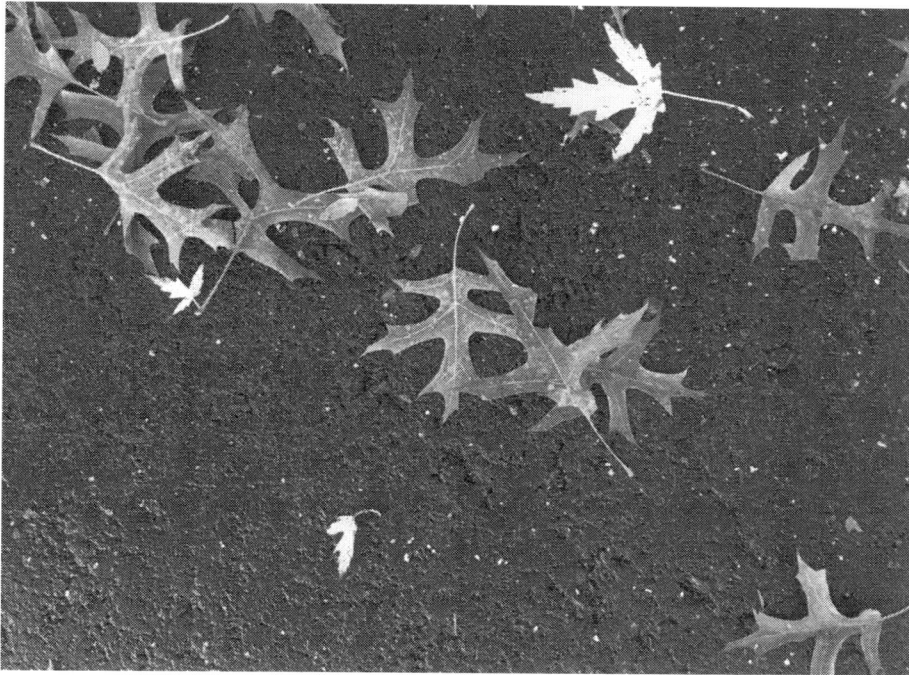

Drift, by Janet Brennan Croft

The Tree That Stood Forever

by Mary Alice Dixon

One day not long ago, as time is measured by trees, a woman wandered fields of thyme and lavender near a small, hard-to-find town. She was a traveler who had become lost looking for home. Her memory was lost, too.

Her name was Seanbhean, which means "old woman" in an tongue largely forgotten these days. But she did not look like an old woman. She looked young, long-limbed, well-muscled, and ample of hip. Her eyes were opal. Her hair was raven-black, except for a single curl of iridescent green that fell across her forehead. And she was lost.

Slowly she walked to the center of the fields where a towering hawthorn tree stood. The tree was so tall its crown seemed to brush away the clouds.

"This feels like home," Seanbhean said, "maybe my memory will come back to me here." The tree smiled.

Under the hawthorn's canopy, Seanbhean built a house of thyme, of lavender and moss. Wide windows opened freely, gladly letting in the breeze. With twigs she laid the floor, with hawthorn leaves she wove the door. But memory did not come.

When night settled in around her, Seanbhean rubbed lavender across her eyes, tucked a sprig of thyme behind one ear, then slept. At midnight she dreamed of a great horned owl high above her in the tree. The owl had emerald feathers and amber eyes that glowed like twin stars in the dark.

When morning came Seanbhean saw clumps of moss had fallen to the ground. She knit them together to make a table, soft and inviting. And she waited. But still, memory did not come.

"Where," she asked the tree, "where is my memory? I can't find my past. Who am I?"

The tree made no answer. But at that moment a weeping fig took root on Seanbhean's table, rising from a broken eggshell.

"Do you know where my memory is?" Seanbhean asked the fig.

In answer, the fig sighed, shedding leaves, shifting its shape. Seanbhean understood. She knew she, too, must change. But she did not remember how. She removed her work boots and her apron, although she knew not why.

As night fell, Seanbhean dressed herself in feathers and combed her hair with talons, gently smoothing out the knots. Waiting, she stood outside her house. Wind sprites whipped across the fields.

"Seanbhean, Seanbhean, your memory will come back," the winds called to her. Seanbhean waited and watched, but memory did not come.

Night after night, Seanbhean dressed herself in feathers and combed her hair with talons. Each night the winds foretold memory's return. But memory did not come.

Seanbhean remembered only that she could not remember anything except her herbs, her berries, and how to dress in feathers. She began to sleep by day. At night she waited, watching the sky through the hawthorn branches, listening to the dream cries of the fields. Each morning, she found that the fig plant had lost more of its once-glossy leaves, and she wept. As her tears watered the hawthorn, the tree grew ever taller.

Then on the first night of summer, Seanbhean made tea from the ripe berries of the hawthorn tree. She drank the tea, crying in despair, "Who am I, who have I been? Who? Who?"

Suddenly she felt the feathers on her dress dance in an old forgotten rhythm. Song filled her throat. Strong winds blew her hair and a wizard appeared, riding the winds, cloaked in midnight, holding a silken map of the sky.

"I followed stars to find you," the wizard said, stepping down from the winds and bowing before her. "I am thirsty for your tea."

He smiled at Seanbhean with sapphire eyes that warmed the night. She returned his smile. Her opal eyes grew amber wise.

"We have met before," she said, remembering.

"We have," he said, kissing her hair.

"My memory," Seanbhean said, "has come home to me.

"My love," she said.

"My love," the wizard answered.

As moonlight broke the sky, Seanbhean took the wizard to her table. All night long they talked, sipping hawthorn tea, recalling days when circuits of the moon were endless, when thyme was evergreen, and nothing was forgotten.

"I remember it all," Seanbhean said, "I remember the tree when the world was a garden. The mother tree from which we branched before we fell. How we leafed in song and spoke in green. How we touched the clouds, flying with feathers of twilight. On a day not long ago."

"Not long ago," the wizard said, "as time is measured by trees."

"This tall tree," Seanbhean said, leaning her head against the hawthorn, "has many stories."

She hooted in happiness and tossed her hair in the wind. Then she lifted her arms and saw that they were wings.

§

On a day not long after this, as time is measured by trees, a girl was born in a small, hard-to-find town. As she grew up she made friends with a young boy who lived nearby. One day, when the girl was gathering thyme and lavender in the fields outside town, the boy came to help her. After filling a large basket, the two walked hand-in-hand to a tall hawthorn tree.

"You know, this tree has stood here forever," she said.

"I know."

"Look," she said, "look, where the horned owl used to nest. Her nest's gone."

"So it is," said the boy, "so it is, for now."

On the ground under the tree they found an empty eggshell, yellowed with age.

"For berries," said the girl, gently lifting the shell. She put a few hawthorn berries into it. "Berries for tea."

"Ah," grinned the blue-eyed boy, wrapping an arm around her waist, "I sure am thirsty." He brushed a lock of hair out of her opal eyes.

"That wild green curl, again," he said, kissing her forehead, "it always comes back. Every time."

"Just like my memory," she laughed, "even my memory of wings."

Seanbhean hooted in happiness, tucked a sprig of thyme behind one ear, and remembered that nothing is lost forever.

Nearby a fig plant took root, watching, unweeping. The hawthorn smiled, remembering its many stories, knowing it would grow many more, becoming ever taller with time, as time is measured by trees.

Reviews

Contributor Publications

Kevan Kenneth Bowkett   *The City of Sapphires*   Sixth Planet Productions   2020
A children's novella in five chapters, this story follows the adventures of Prince Rush and his true love Penny Wiseglass, a humble grocer's apprentice. The Prince must learn the value of following instructions, recognizing good advice, and fulfilling his responsibilities in a magical realm.

S. Dorman   *DuOPolis*   S. Dorman   2019
A group of tech-adept youths discover time-traveling abilities through computer gaming but lack the skill to return to their own exact time and place in this work of speculative fiction that invents a tech jargon as the native language of the children. The time travels take them forward two years and backward to 1900 and to 1769 in the same space.

DC Mallery   *Darksight*   Black Opal Books   2019
Contemporary fiction that imagines the cutting edge of medical science, this novel follows the blind protagonist, Audra, into a terrifying captivity from which she must escape by developing a different sensory power—the darksight of the title—in order to save herself and her guilt-ridden scientist father. The narrative presentation of the experience of blindness is compelling and insightful.

Meg Moseman   *Four Zines of Elsewhere*   Amazon   2020
Some of us will remember the delights of zines, before blogs covered the world, and these four examples, bound as a chapbook, demonstrate how creative this format could be. Combining text, hand-lettering, and drawings, the poems and musings contained within cover a huge emotional range moving toward inner peace.

Joe Murphy   *The Shaman Speaks*   Middle Creek Publishing   2019
This chapbook of fourteen related poems chronicles the life cycle of the poet's imagined magician, healer, and psychopomp, drawing heavily on nature imagery, interiority, and personal growth in free-verse stanzas. Some of these poems have appeared in earlier issues of *The Mythic Circle:* "The Shaman Comforts the Fledgling's Soul," "The Shaman Meets with the Man in the Moon," and "The Shaman's Craft" appeared in issue #37, 2015.

In Memoriam

Ryder Miller, a long-time contributor to *The Mythic Circle*, passed away March 15, 2020. Ryder contributed stories to our journal every year from 2007 to 2019, except for 2013, when he contributed a poem, "The Eye." He died of pancreatic cancer. His brother Ivan commemorated him thus: "He had a rich life with a close and loving family. His mind was a wonder, his heart as tender as they come. He was the gentlest of giants, filled with empathy, unique and creative in his writings and interests. His wide ranging interests in writing, science fiction, literature, and nature provided him with much pleasure and accomplishment. We miss him terribly and we look forward to seeing him again farther along." Best wishes wherever you are, Ryder.

Made in the USA
Las Vegas, NV
24 March 2025